Greek Shadows

Marc Amfreville

Translated by Virginie Actis and John Knych

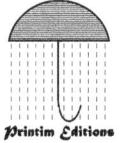
Printim Editions

First published in 2024 by Printim Editions

Printed and bound by TJ Books 2024

ISBN 979-8-9874792-0-9

Copyright © Printim Editions 2024

The right of Marc Amfreville to be identified as the Author of this work has been asserted by him in accordance With the Copyright, Designs and Patents Act 1988.

All rights reserved. No part of this publication may be reproduced,
Stored in a retrieval system, or transmitted, in any form, or by
any means (electronic, mechanical, photocopying, recording
or otherwise) without the permission of the publisher.

Translated from French into English by Virginie Actis and John Knych

This book is a work of fiction. Names, characters, places and incidents are either a product of the author's imagination or are used fictitiously. Any resemblance to actual people, living or dead, events or locales, is entirely coincidental.

First Edition

Originally published as *Ombres Grecques* by Michel Houdiard Éditeur

228 Park Avenue S.
New York, NY 10003
www.printimeditions.com

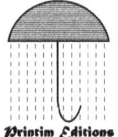

To my grandsons,
Rafael and Sacha

IGOUMENITSA

August 1969

"Can I come into your tent?"

Sitting cross-legged in front of my canvas, I slowly looked up from my book to discover shabby tennis shoes, faded blue jeans, and a flowing, white shirt that had seen better days. He was a surprisingly thin young man with pallid, dark skin. His hair was cropped and of a color difficult to define, between black and chestnut, like the coarse stubble of his beard. It had copper highlights, perhaps from the sunset rays that filtered through the pine needles. The voice seemed almost cavernous to me, and the accent was light, probably Greek. There was something strange in his eyes. As I was slow to answer, he added, "It's going to rain."

I looked at the sky behind him and realized that clouds had suddenly gathered, announcing one of those violent showers that often surprise you after August 15th in the Mediterranean.

"Yes, take shelter, but we'll be a bit tight, my girlfriend is at the cove, she'll surely come running back."

"The cove?"

"The beach, if you like. Between the pines, at the bottom, there are places with sand where you can swim."

We were camping in the wild a few miles from Igoumenitsa. We had one day to wait before catching a boat that would take us to Brindisi and from there back to France. After two of the saddest months in Greece. Okay, taking the road to Athens, through Germany ("next stop Dachau!"), Austria (too clean to be honest), Northern Italy (where even water is not free, bandits!) and Yugoslavia (where we could only afford cabbage and... cabbage) we were not expecting anything cheerful. The coup of the Colonels had taken place two years and a few months earlier and our group of Amnesty International activists had received enough testimonies from recent exiles fleeing the dictatorship to know that the *joie de vivre* of the movie, *Never on Sunday*, was no longer appropriate. We had nevertheless dreamed of being able to have discussions with the inhabitants, if only to inform our group on our return to Paris of what we learned, and if in passing we emptied a few glasses of ouzo while listening to bouzouki, or even learned a few dance steps, our activist goodwill would not be tainted by this. None of this. If it is certain that the living conditions were not as sinister as we had tried to imagine—and had perhaps secretly hoped to find something serious to tell our friends—Greece had seemed to us as sad as Yugoslavia, and perhaps even more so. As if it was all wrapped up in this *nephos* that suffocates the capital, despite the bright light of the islands and the sea. Skyros could well have enchanted us, but we knew that Oropos, the sinister concentration camp, was very close, and that Yaros, a true penitentiary? A penal colony for the political opponents of the Colonels? What remained was the elegance of the cypresses and pines, the meandering alleys where the lime of the houses made us forget the heat, the natural sculptures of the limestone, and the sea, the sea everywhere, at every turn, behind every low dry-stone wall, and more stars than I had seen in twenty years of life... Every night, lying on the sand, soothed by the rising humidity, we both made a wish to each shooting star, and I was sure that, like me, Claire asked for the freedom of Greece.

In Athens, the atmosphere was heavy, the glances furtive, and the silence astounding. It was like a black and white movie. We passed policemen and soldiers at every corner, the landscape was spiked with signs, hastily made monuments and colorful posters in praise of April 21st, 1967 or of an orthodox Greece returned to its Christian culture and values. In the port of Kymi, where we had stopped to take the ferry to Skyros, a huge metal eagle with a particularly cruel look was opening its nationalistic beak, clutching with its talons the message it seemed to be shouting: LONG LIVE THE JUNTA! In the streets of Athens, the crowd, feverish and gray at the same time, completely ignored these two young people, poorly dressed in brightly colored clothes, who were looking for their way.

And then suddenly, the Acropolis! A shock! At the bend of a perpendicular alley, while we were going down Ermou Street from Syntagma Square, the spectacle justified the trip, and we immediately forgot the awful palace of Otto, its evzones a little ridiculous, and the military present everywhere. Heads turned up to see it better. If the heat had not dried my tears in advance and if I had not feared the ridiculousness, I believe that I would have cried. Lost in the maze of Plaka and Monastiraki, we felt almost protected by this benevolent marble vision, overhanging the city like a promise of serenity and freshness found in this overwhelming furnace.

After weeks of our budget only allowing us salads and spaghetti, I remember feeling a little ashamed of the pleasure I took in eating one of those grilled meat skewers sprinkled with lemon, even if, in the first days of our arrival six weeks earlier, I had the impression of discovering what a tomato or a cucumber tasted like...

I squeezed in a little to the left and the stranger crawled inside with difficulty. His body looked sore. Curiously, instead of sitting next to me as I expected, he went to the end of the tent, behind me.

"Do you want something to eat or drink?"

"Some water, if you have it." I turned around to hand him the bottle, and in the darkness, I watched him eagerly drink more than half of it.

"You must have been thirsty!"

No response. The first of those silences that would repeat throughout this conversation and many others that would follow.

"Where are you coming from?"

"From Athens."

"By hitchhiking?"

No answer.

"And where are you going?"

"To Italy."

"The boat to Brindisi, right?"

"Camping is forbidden, what are you going to do if the police arrive?"

Without pointing out to him that he hadn't answered my question, I replied with a laugh,

"The cops came by this morning. They acted tough, but weren't too bad. We told them we were taking the boat tomorrow, they accepted a coffee that we prepared for them in our friends' Volkswagen hippie bus. They made us promise to take down the tent at dawn and they left."

"Would your friends have a place for me?"

"What do you mean? No, I don't think so. There are six of them in their hippie bus, but there are only two of us in an Ami 6 break. We'll be a bit tight, we have three tents in all, we carry the others' because they don't have enough space, but it shouldn't be impossible."

"I can travel in the trunk."

"Are you crazy! Why in the trunk?"

Silence. Then:

"I have no papers."

"And you intend to cross the border hidden in my trunk? But that's completely illegal. We could get in trouble."

Without thinking, I added:

"Tell me why you want to run away."

…

"Look, we'll talk to my girlfriend about it. If she agrees, it's fine with me. But we'll have to give her a good reason."

"I have to leave Greece."

"Are you wanted? You know, we are Amnesty activists from Paris. We came to get information about the dictatorship and to bring news to France. Claire, my girlfriend, will be ecstatic. Sorry… I mean she will surely be interested in your situation and accept to help you. In fact, here she is, at the end of the path."

While wondering why he trusted me so much, and immediately deciding to ignore the question because I was afraid to guess the answer, I got up to meet Claire, who was walking towards the tent.

"I met a young Greek man who wants to be taken across the sea, hidden in the trunk."

"Probably a political opponent. Did you ask him why?"

"He never answers, or at least not directly. He only says that he has to leave the country and that he has no papers. It's going to rain, hurry up."

And she ran off towards our camp. When I knelt down to enter the tent, Claire was already inside.

"Yiorghos, Lucas. Lucas, Yiorghos."

Smiles, Yiorghos's first, exchanged in the darkness. Claire turned to me.

"I told Yiorghos that you had convinced me."

"I know it's dangerous for you," our surprise guest intervened.

"Not at all. If we get caught, we'll say that you had a knife between your teeth and that you threatened us." And she erupted with a big laugh before suddenly becoming serious again. "We don't have a choice because you don't have a choice. And don't thank us, you would do the same for us."

"In Greece, we never thank our friends. If you ask a friend for a cigarette instead of taking it from his pack, he gets angry with you because you created a distance. When you say thank you, you are distancing yourself."

I looked at each of them in turn, with the strange impression that they had known each other all their lives, or at least that they were meant to get along. How could he not have been sensitive to Claire's charm, so graceful, so sparkling? So beautiful too, with her blonde tan and green eyes. And how could she have resisted this dark Greek, who was asking us to take the romantic risk we had always dreamed of in secret? Had I even thought for a second of preventing him from entering the tent? Or to say no to him?

The rain had started, and the drops were pelting against the canvas, making conversation impossible. The darkness was blue and no words were exchanged. When the racket subsided, I offered to go get something to eat. I had spotted a kiosk and a small grocery store on the road before the path that led down to our improvised camp.

When I returned, loaded with three sandwiches, some tomatoes, a bottle of water, sesame pasteli, and a pack of unfiltered Karelia—which Claire preferred to all other cigarettes because of their flattened shape, which she considered "oriental"—I found her outside, leaning against the closed tent. I assumed that Yiorghos was on the other side of the canvas and that they had had plenty of time to talk. She now knew more than I did, and I was eager to ask her some questions.

"Come on, let's take a little walk before we eat?" Claire got up to follow me and a few yards further down the path, I asked her if she had learned anything important.

"No, he didn't tell me anything. We didn't speak. It was very good like that. Have you noticed that he has eyes like an appaloosa?"

"Like what?"

"An appaloosa. You know, those wild horses that are often two colors in cowboy movies. Eyes that are a little crazy and full of light."

"Black?"

"No, more like a chocolate toffee color. Like honey that has been left to burn. But you never notice anything!"

"Me, the eyes of the boys..."

"You're so stupid!"

I thought that the eyes I loved were mostly hers. Green, pricked with small golden points. And so often laughing. Well, so often laughing before the accident.

On the journey from Yugoslavia to Greece, I missed the junction that would have taken us on to a major three-lane road. Completely lost, and of course without a map, we continued along narrow mountain roads, skirting Albania as closely as possible. A few miles from a village whose name I've forgotten, a thunderstorm broke out. We couldn't see five yards ahead of us, and I tried to follow the tail-lights of the car in front of us—the only one we'd seen for dozens of miles. Suddenly, I felt like I was losing control of the steering wheel, as if a tire had gone flat. In fact, this road had just been tarmacked, and under the downpour, the surface hadn't held up. It formed a kind of sticky mud that trapped the wheels and made any movement of the steering wheel ineffective, or at least very uncertain.

"Stay straight!" Claire shouted. "Stay straight, we're going to end up in a ditch!"

In fact, we were driving along a steep precipice. The fall would be over sixty feet, as far as I could tell from the curtain of water crashing against the windows. I felt as if I'd been plunged into an aquarium for scientific experimentation, where a crazy biologist had run the motor of an oxygen pump into a frenzy to test the resistance of two goldfish. The windscreen wipers, broken by the force of the runoff, worked only intermittently. With terror, I realized that the brakes were no longer responding. It's said that in such cases, you see all the images of your life flash before your eyes. Me, none. All I could hear was a muffled thumping rising from my chest and Claire's screams. Suddenly I saw the taillights I'd been following disappear. Had the car gone off the road? My thoughts were racing, I couldn't, I just couldn't put into words what must have happened. And then, a powerful jolt that threw me back against my seat, before hurling me forward in a deafening clatter of sheet metal.

We'd hit a tree. One of the few trees that lined this side of the road above the rocky abyss, spared by the rains. I turned my head towards Claire. Staring, chin trembling, hands clutching her seat, she was livid, but breathing. Gasping, in fact. It wasn't the time, but I thought this girl really did have the most beautiful eyes I'd ever seen. She slowly turned her head.

"I'll never forgive you."

"But it wasn't my fault, it was the tar that melted. I had no control over anything. What would you have done in my place, for God's sake!"

No response. Not that day, nor the following ones when we waited for a mechanic from the nearest town to come and weld a metal plate to the gaping hole in the radiator of my Ami 6, sleeping on straw in a farm where we'd been generously welcomed and fed. Bread, cabbage, and cheese. Never a penny accepted. Very few words exchanged. We didn't speak a word of Serbian. Or was it Macedonian? But each of our hosts' measured gestures was just right, soothing. And to this day, I've kept the image I saw in the rearview mirror of that peasant woman in the green and red kerchief, wrinkled and almost toothless, and her husband with his abundant black moustache, even though his hair had already turned white. Their hands waving in the grey-blue of dawn. Farewell, sometimes, means something.

After hundreds of miles, exhausted by the monotony of national roads, I decided to take a look at the sea. So far, Greece hadn't seemed different enough from Macedonia, and I turned off towards Volos. Claire answered my questions in monosyllables and never spoke to me first. So I decided on my own. I had tried several times to explain to her again what had happened, but in the face of her silence, I had given up. At times, I was furious with her, at others, tender and distraught in the face of what looked like a trauma—a vague, rather boring memory of the clinical psychology textbooks I'd been required to read during the physiotherapy studies I was soon to finish. After all, I was fine, so why not her? And why blame me? Of course, not everyone has the same memories, not everyone has the same story.

After the villages of Damouchari and Makinitsa, we reached Mylopotamos beach. In the middle, a rock divides the stretch of white sand. A little ridiculous, with its mass of limestone topped by a tuft of thorny bushes. But a gap allowed us to cross it. I wanted to see it as an omen of reunion. I was wrong. The only people there at that hour of the morning were a gang of six merry chums frolicking by the water. These Frenchmen we soon learned were Sephardic Jews, who formed a kind of libertarian community on vacation, inspired by the Sixties. Their tanned bodies and curly brown hair matched the scenery so much better than our pale Parisian skin—especially mine, a frankly white russet skin when it wasn't turning bright red in a few minutes under the sun. They mingled naked and uninhibited in the waves and on the sand, and I found it hard to guess which of the three girls and boys were couples. In fact, each boy was more or less in love with the three girls and vice-versa, which gave rise to scenes of intimacy within the first few minutes that made me blush and lower my eyes. After the customary greetings, I was already thinking of going my separate way and leaving them there, but to my great surprise, Claire undressed completely and approached the edge to join them. I inwardly pretexted my fear of sunburn, which made little sense at this time of day, and went to sit down in the shade of a rock.

A few hours later, we were pooling our provisions for lunch on the sand. All six had introduced themselves. Jean-Pierre, the tall, friendly, muscular man, was a bit of a blow-hard. I found Bruno, the smallest of them all, a lot nicer, laughing all the time. As for Samuel, he seemed discreet but warm at the same time. As for the girls, it took me a while not to confuse their first names. Annie was obviously a spontaneous, happy person who loved life and talked non-stop. Nicole, the youngest, marveled at everything—the sand was so white! The sea so turquoise! The waves so high!—and Clothilde, a little further back, looked radiant to me, with her golden skin and big dark-blue eyes. To my great relief, they had all dressed up to eat—"Nudism is no laughing matter under the Colonels after a certain hour," Bruno had joked—and between mouthfuls of food, Claire, suddenly roused from her prolonged torpor, asked everyone questions and told them about our journey. No mention of the accident, however. As we sat in a circle, she managed to avoid my gaze. Other than that, I was feeling better and better, joining in their fits of laughter that broke out at every turn, and if I wasn't sure we shared the same political concerns, I was delighted to hear them talk about the Greeks with respect and a genuine desire to understand them. Clothilde and Samuel had bought themselves a copy of the Assimil method and a conversation manual, and over coffee—they'd even thought of thermoses— they offered to teach us a few basic phrases that they'd recently learned. When I explained to them that I was already doing quite well, having taken courses with Greek exiles in Paris, they immediately decided that we couldn't leave each other, that at the very least, we had to travel a little way together.

And indeed, we had traveled the same path, across the Pelion, Athens, the Sporades, before embarking on a quick tour of the Peloponnese, then Delphi, and on to Igoumenitsa where we had by chance booked the same crossing. Everywhere the same dazzling natural beauty, everywhere the same suppressed sadness as we sensed the prevailing gloom. Everywhere the same hordes of blissful tourists who were moved only by the old stones, sometimes without even admiring the scenery. And yet, as conventional as it sounds, I don't think I'd ever seen a more grandiose landscape than Delphi. The majesty of the mountains stretching as far as the eye could see down to the sea, the silence of the amphitheater amid the deafening song of the cicadas, the scent of thyme and pistachio mastic trees, and above all the fragility of the three columns of the temple of Apollo's oracle. The following night, I dreamed of the Pythia enshrouded in a cloud of sacred smoke: hieratic in her long white robe, her eyes rolled back, her voice hoarse, she promised me love. But soon changed into Cassandra, "A cock hanging from her black throat," as the poet says, she announced that I would remain blind to it. Half-awake, I shouted to her, "I don't believe you, no one has ever believed you." All day long, my head had been buzzing with an inexplicable sadness. *Kaymos*, an untranslatable Greek word. Between desire and sorrow. Nostalgia for what never was, and the pain of loss.

I had mixed feelings about our company. I was happy to know them; I'd even say we'd made friends. Everything seemed easy with them, and I'd gradually seen Claire relax and start talking to me again. And yet, a worry gnawed at me. What if she was unfaithful to me? What if she succumbed to the Mediterranean charm of our new friends? I couldn't quite put my finger on it, but she was particularly close to Clothilde. They spent hours together, a little apart from the others, holding hands or shoulders. Our little gang was amused by the pleasure they took in lathering each other with amber suntan lotion, exaggerating the sensuality of their gestures for the gallery. I wasn't amused. We never talked about what had happened to our couple, even at night when each group was alone in their respective tents. We hadn't made love since the accident. No doubt we needed to let some time pass. There were moments, rather painful ones, when we were close together in our sleeping bags, when I wanted her. Well, I wanted to get back to normal relations. But at other, even more painful times, I realized that I was already used to our distance, and even that I wasn't suffering from it as much as I would have liked.

The sun was waning.

"Why don't we go for a swim?" Claire suggested once we had finished our meal. "The others must still be at the beach. You have to meet them."

"I only swim at night," replied Yiorghos.

"Only at night? Why would you want to do that? You don't look to me like you've got the type of skin to fear sunburn. Even if you are a little pale... As you wish, in any case, we're going. Are you coming, Lucas?"

I followed her down the path.

"He's really hot, don't you think?"

Afraid I'd look too uptight to recognize a boy's good looks, I answered evasively, "I think his nose is too big. He does have a nice smile, but apparently, he hides it. I did notice the size of his canines, though. He looks like a wolf. And he looks so fucking sad!"

"I like that! And it's understandable in his situation. He's about to leave his country, and obviously he has no choice. Do you think we should tell our friends?"

"Listen, the six of them are great. The kind who'd give you the shirt off their backs. I really like them, but it's better not to tell them everything. We'll tell them we met a Greek hitchhiker, that he's going back to France with us because he doesn't have any money for the trip, but we won't say anything about the papers and the crossing in the trunk, okay?"

A few hours later, as we were all sitting on the sand by a branch fire, Yiorghos joined us. Seeing him approach from the beach, I got the impression he was limping. We made introductions. Everyone greeted him kindly and he looked relieved at their welcome. Like every evening, a joint was passed around, offered by the mates, and Yiorghos didn't refuse, although I thought I noticed that he hardly drew on it and later, that he willingly passed his turn. The first time he handed it to me, I took it and sucked down a big drag. Claire laughed at me nicely.

"If Lucas coughs, don't be surprised. It's his first joint all summer. He's always said no to the others." I didn't cough, but after two rounds, my head was already spinning and I started laughing a little too hard and talking nonsense.

"You know, Cassandra is a Trojan. She had no business in Apollo's temple."

The others exchanged surprised glances, and Bruno's laugh broke out, soon to be joined by several others.

"You're wrong," intervened Yiorghos. "The Trojans had the same gods as the Greeks. In fact, Apollo had fallen in love with her. It was he who gave her the gift of… How do you say it in French?" I'd never heard him utter such a long sentence before.

"Clairvoyance," replied Samuel, who'd obviously been studying more than just Assimil.

"Yes. And since she refused his love, and he couldn't take away his gift, he decided that no one would believe her prophecies. At Delphi, I dreamed about it and…"

"Hence the story of the Trojan horse," Nicole interrupted me with a look of amazement, as if she were making a great discovery. "Cassandra had guessed that this horse would ruin the city, but she wasn't believed, so the Trojans let him in, and…"

"Well, that's that. We all know the rest," interrupted Jean-Pierre. "Shall we take a dip?"

It was pitch black, the moon hidden behind the clouds. Everyone got naked and jumped into the water. Even me. I wasn't sure, but I thought I noticed that Yiorghos had done exactly the same. He'd moved away from the light of the flames to undress. Perhaps I wasn't the only prudish idiot in the group.

As we splashed about in the exuberant joy of hashish fumes, the clouds dispersed, and the spectacle of the moon left us in awe. All round. All white. So clear, with the blue contours of its craters perfectly visible. And the trail of its reflection on the sea coming right up to me. To each of us, I imagine. All victims of the same optical illusion. I turned to Yiorghos, who a few seconds earlier had been swimming beside me. He had disappeared.

A moment of panic. What if he'd drowned? I alerted the others, who laughed at my fears, except for Claire who, with a powerful crawl, swam back to shore.

A few minutes later— I swim like a block of iron— I arrived near the fire where the last embers were dying down.

"He's back," Claire told me. "I passed him with his clothes in his hands. He said he'd meet us in the tent. Don't worry, it was dark out. I really wish I had seen him naked, though! Hey, I'm just messing with you, you big dummy... don't get mad!"

"It's not really dark in this moonlight."

"All right, then. I admit it. But I only saw his back."

Our friends had joined us. Jean-Pierre and Bruno started singing with their guitars in front of the tent, as they did every evening. A bit of Brassens, some old French songs, and others in Hebrew, which I found particularly beautiful. At some point, without anyone noticing— except me, no doubt—the tent zipper had come down and Yiorghos had come out on his knees before going to sit soundlessly between Claire and Samuel. Our friends' performance was on point, their six voices crossing, blending, and creating thirds. Nicole in particular had an enchanting tone. When she sang, the slightly naive child disappeared and was replaced by an inspired young woman.

As they all searched for the next song, a joyful gleam passed through her eyes, and she began to hum. It was only a few notes, but the two guitarists recognized the tune at once, and gently began, Bruno plucking a few chords, Jean-Pierre accompanying her in the melody. "*Devant la pierre abandonnée, fleurie de quelques fleurs fanées...*" by Moustaki.[1] An old song with music by Hadjidakis. "*Mais rien ne peut plus ranimer, les cendres mortes enfermées...*"

"But surely this song exists in Greek?" I asked as Nicole finished the three verses, the two boys took up the melody one last time and everyone hummed softly.

As if in a dream, I slowly became aware that one of the chants had turned into words. In a voice that was both husky and soft, Yiorghos had begun to sing. No one seemed surprised. "Η πέτρα είναι ο θάνατος, η πέτρα είναι η ζωή μου"…I knew enough Greek to understand: "The stone is death, the stone is my life." I wanted to translate for the others, but Claire waved me off, which offended me. And then I let myself be carried away by this voice, by the sounds of this strange language, its rhythm where the tonic accents never fall where you expect them to, which makes it so different from Italian or Spanish.

In the tent, without a second thought, I lay down between them. Natural to separate them, right? We were a little tight, but we fit in. Claire was in her comforter, I was in mine, and Yiorghos was all wrapped up in a thin blanket lent to us by our friends. In the dark, I told myself I was probably the only one not asleep. I could feel their heat through the fabric, and I told myself that he should have slept in the middle, because he didn't have a sleeping bag and wouldn't have been so cold. Strangely, I suddenly had the impression of being alone. Like a little boy who has pretended to have a nightmare in order to crawl into his parents' bed and, after feeling warm for a while, can't sleep and feels out of place. Mom's fragrance is too good, he's too old to snuggle up to her chest, and Dad puts him off a bit with his musky smell. Suddenly, they both wake up with a start and throw him out of bed. Curled up on the floor, his stomach feeling hollow, the child hears the last verse of "La Pierre…Tender with love, heavier than remorse…"

"If you don't want to miss the boat…" Jean-Pierre's voice ripped me out of sleep. "I've made you some coffee. Tell Yiorghos that we've gone through our stuff and he can have a shirt of mine and a pair of Samuel's blue jeans, if he wants to change. Also tell him that the local farmer showed us his hose yesterday and mimed explaining that you could use it to shower by hanging it on a branch. Your Yiorghos especially. It won't hurt him, and he'll look better getting into the boat."

I crawled out of the tent, and taking a few steps away, against all the resolutions Claire and I had made, I explained,

"He's going to hide in the trunk. I'll explain later. I don't know if he'll want to shower or take your clothes, but that's nice of you to offer."

"Hide in the trunk? Why would he do that? Okay, I won't ask. I suspected the big-hearted lefties were up to something. Ah, May '68! We demonstrated too, you know. If there's anything we can do to help..."

"Thanks, Jean-Pierre. And thanks for the coffee. Now that I've told you about it, you can tell the others. We'll think about the best way to proceed..."

After the three of us drank our coffee, we saw Samuel arrive. He was bringing the promised clothes, and offered to show Yiorghos the makeshift shower. I was sure he'd say no, but he took the clothes out of his hand and followed without a word.

Claire and I folded up our tent. Between the trees we could see the others dismantling their canvases. When Samuel and Yiorghos returned, our new friend had indeed changed his appearance. Once again, I noticed that he was dragging his leg a little. His new white shirt suited him well, and the blue jeans fit him fine, a little long perhaps, but at least they hid his ridiculous tennis shoes with holes in them. He looked refreshed, happier than the day before, his eyes sparkling. Around the black, amber circles— *amber*, that was the word Claire was looking for. Samuel, on the other hand, seemed strangely mute, as if something had happened. As he turned to head back to his little gang, I caught up with him, leaving Claire and Yiorghos to finish packing.

"Can you show me where the hose is?"

"Okay, come on."

"What's the matter with you? You look pale, like you've seen a snake. Tell me there aren't any."

"Not that I know of."

As we continued, I was insistent: "Don't you want to tell me?"

"I can't tell you, I promised Yiorghos."

"Promised not to tell what?"

"Stop it, please. I can only tell you, after what I saw, that we must do everything we can to help this guy."

"What you 'saw'?"

Samuel gave me a stern look, then his eyes blurred, his chin twitched, he looked like he was going to cry. Awkwardly, I moved closer and hugged him.

"Okay, buddy. Don't tell me... Is this the shower?"

He nodded, walked away to leave me undressing in peace, but suddenly turned around.

"You see, I did the same thing earlier. I showed him the shower and turned back. But suddenly I thought he wouldn't know what to do with his clean clothes. An absurd idea, because he could very well have hung them on a tree. I went back. Already under the water jet, he was singing something different from yesterday. A livelier tune. Like a revolutionary song. He didn't hear me approach. Between the branches, I saw him from behind...I was paralyzed on the spot... He must have sensed my presence, he turned around. Don't force me to describe it, I won't be able to... He approached me, took me by the shoulders with both hands and made me promise not to tell you, then, as if nothing had happened, he asked me if I had any soap."

Samuel's voice choked.

"Lucas...You know better than I do what they say about interrogations in junta prisons. I'm sure he's on the run. If the cops or the military catch him again, he's screwed."

When we rejoined the others, I pulled Claire aside.

"Claire, Samuel has good reason to think that Yiorghos was tortured in prison. Maybe that's why he's limping. I've heard that..."

"I know it. I knew that. I told you I saw his back in the moonlight."

"You told me you couldn't see."

"You never lie, do you? It's not easy to talk about these things. Besides, I thought it might make you lay off. Just look at the state you're in. You're as white as a sheet."

"I'm not laying off. I feel hollow. Like in the nightmares I have all the time..."

She didn't answer, but she kissed me. From the tip of her lips, as a friend.

As planned, as we approached Igoumenitsa, I pulled over to the side of the road, sheltered by a grove of pines. The hippie bus was parked behind me, shielding my car from view. Yiorghos got out of the back seat and slid into the empty trunk, straddling the backrest before curling up as flat as he could under a blanket. I got out of the car, opened the tailgate and, with Claire's help, unfolded a comforter on top of the plaid and, to camouflage our stowaway's shape, piled up a jumble of light objects we'd previously stored between the seats: plastic plates, bathing suits, beach towels, toilet paper, dirty clothes in a ball. Then we covered it all with our second comforter. In the far left-hand corner, I turned over a basin with little holes drilled in it and placed it over Yiorghos's head, which he had left protruding from the plaid and comforters.

If we were stopped by the police, he would have to hide it under the blankets, but in the meantime, he could lift the basin from time to time to breathe easier.

I was about to start the car again when Bruno and Samuel approached.

"Nicole, Annie and Clothilde would like you to get in with them, Claire. With Jean-Pierre at the wheel, you've got nothing to worry about," Bruno joked. Which I didn't find funny. Neither did Claire.

She nodded and walked off without looking back towards the hippie bus. She'd probably already understood the real purpose of the maneuver. Samuel, seeing me puzzled, explained, "We're a bit macho back home, you know?" he explained, "There's no question of letting the girls get caught in any trouble. So we drew lots with Jean-Pierre to see who would come with you."

"And he lost, the dummy fool! Adventure is ours!" laughed Bruno. Then he turned towards the back. "We can't do without you, Yiorghos," he added in a barely more serious tone. "Especially now that you're clean!"

Yiorghos didn't answer right away. I'd imagined him anxious, as anyone would be in that situation. But suddenly his voice, muffled by the basin, reached us.

"Δεν ελπίζω τίποτα, δεν φοβάμαι τίποτα, είμαι ελεύτερος."

"What's our submarine diver saying?" asked Bruno.

I repeated, articulating distinctly.

"Then elpizo tipota, then fovame tipota, ime elefteros. He says he hopes for nothing, fears nothing, he is free."

"This is the epitaph engraved on Kazantzakis's tombstone in Heraklion," explained Samuel. "Something to think about."

"Well, it's certain that where he is, he doesn't have much to hope for or fear," commented Bruno. "It's not very funny. I prefer 'Freedom or Death' as a motto. That's the title of one of his novels, isn't it, Mr. Know-it-all?"

I thought of the Kazantzakis song: "The stone is death, the stone is my life," throat knotted. But as I turned to the trunk, echoing the cry of Bouboulina, a heroine of the Greek War of Independence, I launched with gusto: "Ἐμπρὸς παιδιά!" Forward, children! A way of giving others the courage no one seemed to lack. Or to silence my fear. My fears.

Of us being caught? Of him getting arrested? Or of just losing him altogether?

The boat left at 11:30 p.m., so we had to be there two hours before. It was already a dark night when we arrived just after 9:00 p.m., in sight of the ferry moored alongside a concrete quay below the road, but I shouted to Yiorghos to hide. In front of the customs hut where a Greek flag was flying, I moved the car slowly forward to join the long line of vehicles that had formed parallel to the shore, but weren't moving. Illuminated by two streetlamps, a red-and-white barrier was lowered to the right of the hut on the water's edge, but the unusual thing was that, further to the right, there was nothing to prevent access to the loading area reserved for trucks. The hippie bus was right behind us, and I waved to Jean-Pierre and Annie in my rearview mirror, not sure they could see me in the dark.

Despite the hard day's waiting and the palpable tension in the car, Bruno was his usual mocking self.

"If they look like they're going to stop us, don't bother tearing down the barrier. Just drive around it and straight ahead."

The queue was moving slowly, and we soon understood why. The two soldiers on duty not only asked for the papers of the vehicles and their occupants, each at a window, but also had to seek the approval of their superior before signaling each driver to move on. The latter would raise his arm, looking martial but fortunately unconcerned, and the car could head for the ferry where, with a loud whistle, a naval officer would show the way to the bowels of the hold. Other sailors were waiting for cars, waving their arms authoritatively and showing them where to park. At the back, if a car was going to Brindisi as we were; if the car was going to get off at our only stopover, Corfu, they'd go on the right and left gangways. I wondered for a while how they kept track of destinations, until another company employee came knocking on my window—which made me jump in my seat— and asked me in English where we were going. When Samuel, in the back seat, replied, "To Brindisi, my friend," the sailor stuck the corresponding sign on the windscreen. Mockingly, Bruno pinched my cheek before asking:

"Have you counted how many cars are in front of us? I'll tell you: twelve. That's perfect!"

"Why do you say that?"

"Because, look," Samuel explained. They're searching every fourth car. The first, then the fifth, the ninth, and so on. So not us. The hippie bus. But we don't care about that."

I took a deep breath and put the car into first. Apparently, everything was fine. When I reached the soldier's level, Bruno and I rolled down our windows and showed our papers and those of the car. The superior's eminent sign and off we went. In the rear-view mirror, I saw Jean-Pierre and Annie do the same. I moved forward a few yards and suddenly perceived from where I stood an inexplicable confusion aboard the Volkswagen. Shouting voices. The sliding door creaked open at the rear. Claire got out of the car, seemed to be parleying and soon arguing with the soldiers who were bellowing back. What could be going on? Samuel, turning to the rear window to try and understand what was happening, whispered to Yiorghos,

"Don't worry. We're through. They're checking the hippie bus."

No response from Yiorghos. I could imagine his anguish. Samuel put his hand on my shoulder, Bruno his on my knee. A sailor approached my car and beckoned me forward. I showed him the stopped hippie bus: "Friends, φίλοι…" He became exasperated, fidgeted and started whistling again. I tried to ignore him, but he stuck his head very close to the window I had just raised, and alternated invective and whistling until I started the engine again. I didn't know whether to keep Yiorghos out of danger or wait to find out what was happening to Claire. Samuel advised me to drive forward a few yards, but I remained stunned for who knows how long. Claire finally headed towards us, escorted by a soldier. The other barked something. Sweat was on my forehead. The officer left his pedestal and approached too. I rolled down the window. He addressed me in French,

"The lady says you have her passport." I took a deep breath, reached into the glove compartment, found the passport and presented it to him. "Why isn't the lady in your car?"

"Because they're angry," Bruno answered, "A lovers' quarrel," he said while banging one fist against the other. "It's nothing serious."

The officer nodded. I looked at Claire, who looked away. Playing up the quarrel, no doubt. The man then gave a sign to one of the soldiers who went to the back of the car and opened the boot. I watched him in the mirror. With a jerk, he lifted the comforter, looked at the mess we had carefully organized, grimaced, pushed the comforter back and closed the tailgate.

I finally managed to park the Ami 6 between two metal pillars although the vociferous sailors who were supposed to be guiding us filled me with panic. We got out of the car, without daring to give a word of encouragement to our stowaway. Past the metal passageways, we emerged from the belly of the whale into a surprisingly luxurious setting. White lights, thick carpets and gleaming woodwork. Of course, we didn't have the money for a cabin—Claire and I didn't, anyway— and we found ourselves on deck, having climbed multiple increasingly steep staircases and passed through increasingly heavy doors. The coolness surprised me after the damp mugginess of the hold, but the view of the harbor, at last, the lights of the city and the surrounding hills, comforted me. We were out of danger, the last vehicles were coming aboard, and soon we were reunited with Jean-Pierre and the girls. Claire was in a foul mood. Annie and Nicole looked nervous. Samuel and Clothide, as always, said little. Bruno tried to lighten the atmosphere. Imitating a coarse German accent, he addressed Claire,

"Okay mee-ss, you vanted to traval vit-out pass-a-port?"

But the joke fell flat. Like the others, no doubt, I was thinking of Yiorghos curled up in the trunk, suffering from the heat and lack of air. Claire broke the silence after making sure there was no one within earshot but us.

"They checked the tickets and papers when we got on. Now I don't think there's any risk. It's pitch black on this deck anyway. We'll get him out of the car and keep him in the middle of us. No one will notice a thing."

"Not before Corfu," interrupted Jean-Pierre. "We've got to get out of Greek territorial waters first."

"He's right, Claire," insisted Samuel, and I was happy that he said it for me. But that didn't stop her from glaring at me before sulking away from the group.

We watched the sailors cast off and the deck slowly rise. I thought of a coffin closing, and imagined the complete darkness that must have invaded the hold.

A few hours later, as we huddled together on the wooden benches to protect ourselves from the wind and humidity, the ship's siren sounded, and the crowd of passengers rushed forward to admire Corfu as they passed the command post. However, it didn't take a rocket scientist to guess that the ferry was about to turn around and head back towards the port, spitting out the cars that would stop on the island and perhaps swallowing a few more.

Suddenly, Jean-Pierre signaled that he wanted to talk to us.

"We'll take advantage of the movement to go back down into the hold. We don't all have to go. Lucas, you're coming with me, because it's your car. If anyone asks for anything, you'll say you went to get some medicine you forgot, and I'll tell them I'm a doctor and your girlfriend needs it."

After several interminable minutes, as passengers could only descend the stairs in single file, or nearly so, we reached the iron door set with huge bolts that opened up onto the hold. Obviously, it remained open, the threshold barred only by a chain that a sailor had just removed. The few vehicles going down to Corfu were parked as close as possible to the exit. Jean-Pierre and I ducked between the rows of other cars to get up to mine. I feared that someone would catch us, and my pulse had already started to race. From a distance, I spotted the Ami 6 with its caramel bodywork, unmistakable even under the light of the electric bulbs. We crawled up to it, I opened the tailgate, whispering:

"It's us, Yiorgho, don't be afraid."

No response. I lifted the basin, the blanket, the comforters. No one was there. Yiorghos had disappeared. I turned to Jean-Pierre, who looked as dumbfounded as I was. We turned back. This time a sailor was guarding the passage, and without a word, I showed him my car keys, a first-aid kit I'd had the presence of mind to take from the boot, and Jean-Pierre quickly uttered the words, "Doctor, doctor," pointing to his chest, as if in a hurry.

We climbed back on, four at a time, against the current, as fast as the last of the passengers heading down to Corfu would let us. We met up with our friends on deck in a dimly lit corner. Yiorghos was among them, and they all surrounded him solicitously, as much to keep him out of sight as to express their delight at the success of our venture.

"But how..."

"It was me who went looking for him," interrupted Claire. "I figured there mustn't be much air left in your roller jar. You were taking too long to make up your mind. I had the spare key, so..."

"Any problems with the sailor?" I asked, trying to hide my anger.

"No problem at all. I unbuttoned my blouse and while he had a good look, Yiorghos was able to pass unnoticed."

I almost choked with rage.

"I don't believe you," objected Jean-Pierre. "Nobody doubts your charms, but if I'm not mistaken, that's a t-shirt you're wearing."

"And t-shirts don't have buttons," added Bruno.

"You're right not to believe me. The truth is, when we passed by, the sailor wasn't yet at his post. We passed him in the first basement and pretended to be looking for directions, turning around so he'd think we were going down too. He didn't ask us anything, Yiorghos can tell you."

"Nothing at all."

No one seemed to want to provoke an argument. Least of all, me, even if Claire's solo expedition was a risk I considered completely insane, and this ultimate bravado highly inappropriate.

Yiorghos was clearly exhausted by his latest incarceration. Even in this semi-darkness, he looked even paler than when he first appeared in front of my tent.

"I need some air now."

And he moved away from the group towards the bow of the boat, where there were no more passengers, all busy admiring the harbor lights on the other side. As if fearing he might fall overboard but not wanting to bother him, Bruno and Samuel followed him a few paces away. They were right to do so, because even though the ferry had not yet set sail and was therefore barely pitching in the harbor basin, Yiorghos began to stagger during the last few yards separating him from the rail. Samuel and Bruno rushed over, grabbed him under the armpits and helped him hold on to the rail. Then they each put an arm around his shoulders. I couldn't hear them from where I was standing, but I thought they made a fine triptych, with Yiorghos staring out to sea, turning his back on the last island of the country he'd left behind, his two supporters with their heads slightly bent towards him. Although a non-Christian, I thought of a crucifixion, and found it moving.

We shared the blankets and comforters that our friends had thought to take from their hippie bus, while Claire and I had left ours in the car to hide our passenger. We were in neatly lined-up rows: first the two couples—during our journey, I'd come to understand who was with whom—first Bruno and Nicole, then Jean-Pierre and Annie; in the middle Yiorghos, then Samuel and Clothilde—who weren't dating but adored each other, then Claire and me, us not quite knowing where we stood. At the very edge of the improvised dormitory, completely frozen, I didn't manage to fall asleep until two or three in the morning. I admired the sky: the stars were trembling, none of them shooting stars. I couldn't make a wish. I rehearsed in my mind the boat trip to Brindisi, the border between Italy and France, our arrival in Paris. All the difficulties that awaited us and might spoil a return trip that I wasn't even looking forward to. *What fun you have worrying*, Claire often said. All the same, the danger was behind us. Yiorghos wasn't really out of the woods yet, but he soon would be. We were succeeding. Why couldn't I feel calm, then? Why the occasional throbbing in the hollow of my throat since Igoumenitsa, and especially since the moment I'd seen Yiorghos on the deck earlier? As if I were becoming intermittently aware of his vulnerability, or of our responsibility. Or both.

When I woke up at dawn, most of the others were still asleep, but there was nobody on my right. Yiorghos, Claire, and Clothilde were gone. I walked the deck looking for them. The sea was sky blue and the sky pale. Italy was not yet in sight, but behind us, the sun was already rising, a perfect disc that colored the foam of our wake with orange reflections. I wanted to see more, to let the wind whip me, even though I wasn't very warm. Behind the top deck there was a ladder pressed against the wall. I started to climb the rungs and saw that it led to a small platform of which only the end could be seen from our deck; as I cautiously climbed up, watching where I put my feet, I suddenly saw Clothilde's ankles, then her legs descending from the perch where I had thought to spend some time alone.

As she crossed paths with me, halfway up, she turned towards me, and I had the impression she blushed.

"Do not go up," she said. "You get all the smoke in your face up there and you don't see any better than below."

"I still feel like it."

I continued my climb. When my shoulders passed the level of the floor, I raised my head. Against the light, on the background of the rising sun, their dark silhouettes cutting against the blue stretching to the horizon, I saw them.

I don't know how I didn't fall off the ladder. I clung to the uprights and hoisted myself up until my knees reached the last step. Standing in the gusts that slapped my face, I waited for them to notice my presence. Yiorghos was the first to see me, he disentangled himself from Claire's arms and took a few steps towards me, hands spread, palms towards the sky. I descended as quickly as I could and ran back to join the group, thinking that it would take him a while to come down and that in front of the others, he would not dare to explain.

Clothilde came out of the shadow of a pillar. She stopped my run by grabbing my two arms, pulling me behind a lifeboat; there, we could not be seen, and the wind was less deafening.

"Don't be mad at them, Lucas. I was up there before them, curled up behind a parapet to protect myself from the wind. They didn't see me. I know how it happened. It was a gust that pushed them. They almost lost their balance walking towards the railing. Yiorghos collapsed, it always seems like he limps a bit and is unsteady on his legs; Claire caught him. They fell into each other's arms. From a distance, it seemed to me that it was by chance that they…"

"By chance! But how could he do that to me? It's me who saved him, for God's sake!"

"Not alone, Lucas."

"We're arriving in Brindisi, and I'm going to report him! The bastard!"

"You won't do that! I forbid you!"

This tone of authority, the urgency in her voice surprised me. Clothilde was always so calm. So gentle.

"I would really like to know how you plan to stop me."

"It's going to hurt you, but you're forcing my hand. It's true, it wasn't by chance. Anyway, two people never kiss 'by chance.'"

"He took advantage of the situation, is that it? Help me up, and bam, while I'm holding on to you, I hug you and kiss you. The bastard!"

"No, Lucas. It was she who embraced him, who took him by the neck, who drew his head toward hers, she who kissed him."

"He didn't seem to be struggling when I caught them."

"I think he was as taken aback as you, that he didn't know how to get away. And if you want my honest opinion, she didn't think about it either. It must have been an impulsive act, a rush…The sunrise, the exhilaration of having succeeded in his escape, the aftermath of danger. Annie and Nicole, those silly girls, say he is irresistible. They think with his wild eyes, he looks like Omar Sharif in *Lawrence of Arabia*. Sheik Ali Ibn, I don't remember what. He's not my type at all. Everything about him is too much: a nose too big, cheeks too hollow, cheekbones too prominent, and then he's too skinny and I'm sure he's too hairy. Plus, I find him strange, even though I can't explain why. I don't think Claire had a love at first sight. She would have told me before. We're very close you know, even if we've only known each other for a short while."

Yiorghos eventually found us. Clothilde discreetly moved away.

"I apologize. All this time in prison, without a woman. Claire was too beautiful in the light. I lost my head. It's my fault, I kissed her by force."

"Clothilde saw you. That's not what she told me."

"…"

"It's not the first time she acts like a tease. She says it doesn't count. That since May '68, no one belongs to anyone anymore. That she is free with her body!"

"And you?"

"Me, I'm faithful, but I don't have to force myself. I care about her, you understand? I too find that jealousy is ugly, that fidelity is outdated. So here we are, that's how it is, I'm always jealous, and never unfaithful. And moreover, now, I don't even know if we are really together. She has barely talked to me since we met the others. I always feel like she's avoiding me. Why did you lie to me earlier by saying it was you who…"

"I didn't lie. I don't really know where I stand anymore. And then, it was better for you," he replied, looking at me intently. "Clothilde shouldn't have…"

"She was afraid I would denounce you."

"She knows you wouldn't do that."

"So?"

"I don't know. But you, you must feel it…"

A few hours later, we were all sitting on the wooden benches while Yiorghos was leaning against the rail. His back was turned to us and he was smoking one cigarette after another. I watched him out of the corner of my eye. Quite foolishly, I thought that his white shirt and blue jeans resembled the Greek flag snapping in the wind on the middle deck. And even more foolishly, for me who always found flags a bit ridiculous, I felt a strange emotion take hold of me. This trivial nationalism of the colors hoisted on the mast suddenly made sense. As if, at that moment, I had shared a bit of the pain of his exile. I wanted to get up, to rush over to Yiorghos, to tell him that everything was forgotten, that there were so many more important things. My jealousy was ridiculous… I had to apologize.

Annie's joyful shout stopped me. The awning of the kiosk, from which a wisp of black smoke had been escaping through a squat chimney, had just been lifted.

"I'm starving, it looks like they've fired up a grill, and I smell good little skewers. Doesn't that tempt anyone?"

"Go ahead, Annie, order for everyone, we'll join you when it's ready," Bruno called out, flaunting his usual machismo without apparent effort.

"I'll come help," Nicole offered. "Ah, men!"

I approached the kiosk thinking Annie might need a translator and also feeling a little stung by Nicole's remark. There was a cook in an apron, crowned with a cap meant to be white, half-turned so as not to take his eyes off the sizzling skewers. Strands of grey hair stuck to his forehead, and his cheeks crinkled under a greasy smile that was meant to be welcoming, which mysteriously vanished when his eyes landed on Annie's t-shirt. At first, I didn't understand why. Without questioning further, I confirmed the order with my friend,

"Nine skewers in pitas with tomatoes, onion, and white cheese?"

"Yes."

I began to translate, quite pleased to showcase my linguistic skills. But Annie seemed to tense up. Embarrassed, she stopped me with a hand gesture. And at first, I thought it was because she would have preferred that I leave Yiorghos, who had joined us, the opportunity to be of service.

"Yiorghos, ask him what kind of meat it is. Several of us..."

"Pork, Miss," the cook interrupted, whom we could have assumed, given his contacts with tourists from all countries, spoke French fluently.

Annie furrowed her brow. The seller burst into laughter.

"So, the Miss doesn't want it, I understand," he added with a sardonic air and a malicious glint in his eyes, pointing to the gold Star of David shining on Annie's neck, which I felt like I was noticing only at that moment. "You don't eat pork, and of course, you don't like to waste money. But I took the order, and I warn you, you will have to pay."

I wondered if I understood correctly. I was distracted by a thought that perhaps wasn't so far-fetched: how was it possible that after the deportation of the Jews from Corfu, not so long ago after all, there were still Greek anti-Semites? Since I have a bias for Greeks, I immediately decided he must be Italian, like a good part of the crew.

Yiorghos, on the other hand, had been distracted by nothing. With a leap, he approached the counter. I saw his hand grab the edge, his body rise diagonally in front of the Formica paneling, and his other fist shoot forward.

"Την Παναγία σου..."

Annie and Nicole screamed. The boys rushed over. The cook was holding his nose, but oddly, he continued to smile. Bruno and Samuel wrapped their arms around Yiorghos and pulled him back. Samuel handed me three-hundred drachma notes without a word. He didn't need to explain. Overcoming the disgust that the pile of fat inspired in me and the nausea caused by the trickle of blood dripping from his nostrils, I stammered,

"Our friend isn't himself. He drank too much last night and is seasick. It's making him lose his mind. Here, I'll pay for the souvlakia. Here's a hundred drachmas."

Each skewer was worth ten, already an exorbitant price compared to those on dry land.

"Keep the change."

The man grabbed the bill, while keeping his eyes on the other two I was holding in my hand. I spread one out on the counter and slid it towards him, keeping a finger on it.

"Let's forget it, shall we?"

He, in turn, placed a grimy-nailed index finger on the bill.

"Alcohol and bandages are expensive," he replied, staring straight into my eyes.

The third bill followed the first two, and he pocketed it all with a satisfied air.

I joined the others who had gathered at the other end of the bridge, except Claire and Clothilde who had disappeared.

"Well, what a right hook you've got there! But how did you manage with your legs? Usually, you can barely stand on them. You looked like a wildcat. 'Supple and ferocious like a tiger,' that's what they say in Costas Gavras's film *Z*. I saw it in March."

"You know as well as I do, Doctor Sultan," Jean-Pierre explained, "a shot of adrenalin can make you forget the most severe pain for a moment. At the hospital, I once saw a patient who'd been operated on the day before get up and slap a nun who'd seen fit to lecture him about how he had no one to blame but himself and alcohol abuse if his spleen burst. The patient jumped out of bed, and bing, a knuckle sandwich!"

"You're out of your mind, Yiorgho, imagine if that guy had filed a complaint and the sailors had asked for your ticket and papers," I protested, my voice trembling with the anger I'd managed to contain until then.

"That's exactly why I think he's a hero," Nicole exulted.

"A hero, perhaps, an unconscious man, no doubt, but a friend, for sure!" replied Samuel with an emotional smile.

"I've been telling you from the start that he's a brother! By the way, did you see his nose? I think it looks like mine," laughed Bruno. "I wouldn't call that a Greek nose!"

"One cliché after another, and he thinks he's funny," Annie sighed gently.

"What did you say to him, Yiorghos, when you punched him in the face?" asked Jean-Pierre.

...

"He said, 'Tin Panayia sou,'" I replied in his place. "In Greek, one of the most common insults is a name in the accusative, your mother, your sister, your family, even your church, or in that case, your Virgin. Implied in front of the word is the verb 'ghamo,' something like 'Fuck' in English."

"Why do you say 'Fuck' in English, in French it would get stuck in your throat?" joked Bruno. "What's the accusative?"

"It's the case of the direct object complement, you ignoramus," replied Samuel, no doubt to save me from being the only pedant on board.

"You pronounce Greek gamma very well, Lucas, that's rare," intervened Yiorghos, perhaps anxious to put an end to his own silence.

"Gamma, that's like our G, isn't it?" asked Nicole.

"A 'g' with an 'h' after it that blows, that rasps a little against the palate. It's a beautiful letter and you French, well most of you, can't hear it."

Blushing at the compliment, I wanted to appear modest:

"I've been practicing a lot."

"To pronounce Yiorghos properly!" exclaimed Nicole, clapping her hands and achieving a very honorable gamma, without suspecting that she had hit the nail on the head.

At dawn, we arrived in view of Brindisi, and despite all my apprehensions, disembarking and passing through customs went smoothly. We were among the first to descend to the holds, and while Claire and I pretended to arrange the trunk, Yiorghos had once again slipped under the blankets. It was an unnecessary precaution because we weren't even stopped by customs officers. Three days remained for us to be in Paris by Sunday, and while Claire and I still had time before returning to classes and internships, Jean-Pierre and Bruno were expected at their hospital first thing Monday morning. The other students' university term wouldn't start for another month and a half, but everyone had good reasons to return home. Without needing to discuss it, we all agreed to cross Italy as quickly as possible, and the main reason was that we were eager to get Yiorghos to safety in Paris. We had also decided to head west after Modena to reach Genoa, and from there, towards Ventimiglia and France, rather than going through Switzerland. The route would have been shorter, but it would have meant crossing two more borders.

Once out of the city, already on the highway, we stopped at a service station to free our 'prisoner.' Yiorghos seemed groggy again when he left his hiding spot, and to my surprise, he walked slowly toward the hippie bus. Claire, who had remained in the Ami 6 until then, followed him, and I watched them from a few yards away get into the camper van, Claire in the front, next to Jean-Pierre, Yiorghos in the back with the others. Perhaps sensing my discomfort, Bruno responded with his usual humor.

"If your car were less ugly, maybe you'd have more volunteers."

Samuel, without a word, came to sit next to me. Before closing the door, however, he turned to Clothilde with a silent invitation, but she did not respond.

The arid landscape along the Adriatic through Puglia might have been beautiful, but my eyes were fixed on the road and my jaws ached from clenching them. From time to time, I would look at the back of the hippie bus leading the way, imagining the light-hearted exchanges, the joy of shared songs, Claire relieved not to be with me, Yiorghos getting to know his new friends. In fact, all I saw were the backs of Bruno and Nicole on the rear bench. So Yiorghos must have been sitting in the middle, between Clothilde and Annie. At least he wasn't next to Claire.

Samuel was far from the most talkative of the group, and I could tell he was making an effort to start a conversation.

"I'll take the wheel as soon as you feel tired."

"No problem for now. Let's try to make some headway, and we'll switch in an hour or two." Ten minutes later, I forced myself to speak, despite the overwhelming heat, primarily to keep from brooding:

"How do you all know each other? Have you been friends for a long time?"

"We were in the E.I. together."

"The E.I.?"

"The Israelite Scouts. The E.I., that's our scouts. Well, not related to the French Scouts. Nothing paramilitary, you see. Mostly friends getting together, going for hikes on the weekends, summer camps, and also sticking together to support Israel. Especially since the Six-Day War..."

"I've heard about it."

"We all met there when we were kids. Well, everyone except Clothilde. She encountered Annie three or four years ago at the Cité Universitaire, and otherwise, she has nothing to do with us... I mean, she comes from a big Protestant family. By the way, if you don't mind me asking, where are you from? What's your family name?"

"Are you asking if I'm Jewish?"

"Yes, it's something we've all wondered about, actually."

"Well, yes, I mean...no. My name is Landau. Landauer, actually, but my father had the last two letters dropped when he came of age. He's Austrian Jewish, but he's always hidden it. His parents were deported, and after the war, he wanted nothing more to do with all that. As if he'd spent his life fearing the next round-up. With a name like that, it was easy not to talk about it. The French pronounce it as if it was a stroller. And then he married my mother, who is not Jewish. A militant secular schoolteacher. So you see, it's complicated for me. I was raised a thousand miles away from all that culture. With the goys, as you say, I always feel like saying who my father is, where he comes from, the Holocaust is his story, and therefore, it's mine too. But for the Jews, because of my mother, I know I'm not one of them. It's like a double-edged sword. In the end, I belong nowhere."

"I can imagine that it wasn't easy every day, indeed."

"My turn to ask a question. You don't have to answer, of course. You and Clothilde...?"

"Not simple either. I think I fell in love with her the first time Annie brought her around. But she made it clear she preferred we stay friends. Listen, it's not a secret, but I would have preferred she told you herself. How to put it? Clothilde prefers girls. She says she has a lot of affection for me, that she would like us to always see each other, but..."

I thought back to when Clothilde had described Yiorghos to me on the boat. It seemed she was genuinely repulsed by him. By his hair, in particular, although in reality, he didn't have that much of it. Then I remembered those moments on the beaches when, with Claire, they would leisurely apply suntan lotion to each other. Two young lionesses on the sand, playful, sensual... Her long, fine yet robust hands lingering on her shoulders, her thumbs drawing circles on her back, her bronzed skin irresistibly approaching Claire's paler hue. Suddenly, I thought I understood what Yiorghos had meant by his "You must feel it." Clothilde had wanted me to know that Claire initiated the kiss so that I would hold it against her, that we would break up, and then, who knows, that she would let herself be consoled... I was a little ashamed to attribute such Machiavellian calculations to her, and I wasn't even sure if she had articulated them to herself, but obviously, she was attracted. As for Claire, I knew her well enough to guess that she probably didn't even suspect her new friend was interested in her in that way. And I knew her well enough to be sure that such an adventure would never tempt her.

"And are you unhappy?"

"Not really anymore. At the beginning, yes, but I've found peace now. We're really close, you know? And then, I tell myself that maybe one day...

That she's not Jewish, I don't care about that, too bad for the parents. And you, you should also not care about what others think. What matters is what you feel you are."

Throughout the entire trip in Italy, Yiorghos only got into my car once, and it was for a very short stretch. He didn't talk much, if at all. So, I gathered up my courage, and with as casual an air as possible even though the question had been nagging me since Igoumenitsa—I dared to ask him why he had been arrested, and curiously, he agreed to answer me. But as if he had given all he could, as if he feared I would ask more, at the next stop near Bologna, he went back to his place in the hippie bus.

We stopped for the night in Arenzano, a small town next to Genoa. We decided to sleep under the stars without setting up the tents, at the very end of the volcanic beach lined with tamarisk, beyond the last houses. I couldn't shake the feeling that Yiorghos was avoiding me but, to be honest, I must say that he seemed to have walled himself up in a bastion of solitude that no one could penetrate. As he sat a little apart at the edge of the water, I approached, knelt in the black sand a meter from him, but we didn't speak. In the moonlight, his profile was silhouetted against the sky, and for the first time in days silence didn't seem like a curse to me. I felt, as I had on the boat watching the Greek flag, that he was allowing me to hear something of the pain of exile. I heard it, but it took an effort to understand it. I felt no attachment to any place. I could have left France forever without regrets. Yet, like a blinking light, by striving to put myself in his place, I began to glimpse what it feels like to tear oneself away from a country one loves. Perhaps because four centuries of Turkish occupation had shaped for the Greeks a relationship with their land that is both an anchoring and a dream of freedom, their nationalism seemed understandable. In France, July 14th and all the cock-a-doodle-dos had always seemed ridiculous to me. In Greece, I had been surprised to find myself moved hearing the national anthem, or rather seeing the fervor with which the people listened to it, or even how the religious ceremonies united and transported them. Where had my belief gone that religion is the opium of the people? My mother would have turned in her grave had she been close to going there. And then, even though I knew that man is capable of becoming attached to an ugly patch of earth—I thought of the mining towns, for example—the beauty of the country was surely not unrelated to the Greeks' passion for their land. They talked about it all the time. As if they needed to convince us. Really unnecessary. I had loved the intensity of the blue everywhere, the sea, the color of the sky, the aridity of the rocks…We were crossing Italy, but already, the light was not the same. It was blond, soothing. There, the light strips you bare, it sandblasts you. It wounds you. Two months in Greece, and I already missed it. I dreaded Paris, the rain, the absence of music. Above all, through my little end of the telescope, I could glimpse what Yiorghos was going to feel. My throat tightened, I had to break this silence.

"Do you not speak to me anymore?" I asked. "Are you mad at me?"

"Why do you say that? It's myself I'm mad at."

"I got angry too quickly."

Just at that moment, Bruno approached.

"Hey you lovebirds! Are you coming to eat? We found some takeout pizzas. And they're getting cold."

"Not ham, I hope," Yiorghos said softly, and all three of us burst out laughing.

After Savona, just before Ventimiglia, Claire got into the Ami 6 for the first time and Yiorghos went back into the trunk. I was nervous again, but we weren't stopped at any of the successive border checkpoints. We were in France, we had made it. Claire shouted with joy and kissed me. A big smack on the cheek that warmed my heart. We still waited until Menton to take a break and free Yiorghos. Then, Samuel offered to drive, Claire joined the hippie bus, Yiorghos took her place in the passenger seat and I lay down in the back to nap, lulled by the boys' singing as they discovered a shared repertoire of songs. We stopped again to sleep in an olive grove near Orange. Scrubland, slate-colored hills, cicadas: it was Greece, but it was no longer Greece. I closed my eyes. Yiorghos was walking away from the shore, standing between the waves. His back was smooth, it surprised me. While he should have been out of his depth, he walked straight ahead, without looking back. The water was already at his neck and he kept moving forward. I called his name to warn him of the danger, and in my dream, my shout woke me up. The moment after, Claire, Yiorghos, and I were running among grape-laden vines, clad only in vine leaves, the wind blowing in gusts, and while they both seemed joyful, I was anxious and feverish.

The next morning, I told my dream to Clothilde, who was traveling next to me. I wanted her, armed with her psychology studies, to interpret it, all the while bracing myself against her analysis. She would probably talk about my fear of seeing Yiorghos drown, my desire to erase his suffering, and I didn't need her for that. I wanted her to explain my anxiety in the second part of the dream. Against all expectations, she burst out laughing, and adopting the caricatured tone of a psychic-turned-oracle, as indeed I often imagined her, she asked me:

"What do you think of that strong wind, Mr. Landau?"

...

"A gust could well tear off a vine leaf. Or another, right?"

I found the question stupid, and especially out of place. I was almost embarrassed for her. The wind was just a detail in my dream. I would have done better to keep quiet. Yiorghos was drowning and she was talking about gusts in the vineyard. Just wind, all of it, I thought, pleased with my own humor. Paris awaited us with a whole lot of serious problems. It was time to return to reality.

PARIS

Sunday, August 31st, 1969

We had arrived in Paris via the Porte d'Orléans. At the foot of the recently inaugurated statue of Leclerc, we had parked for a moment to say goodbye. We exchanged addresses and phone numbers—for those of us who had them. The friends got back into their bus and headed towards the southern suburbs where they all lived. Samuel with his parents in Sceaux, Nicole with hers in Bagneux, Jean-Pierre and Bruno in the two-room flat they shared in Bourg-la-Reine, Clothilde and Annie in rooms at the Cité Universitaire, Croix de Berny.

"I'll give you a week to rest," Jean-Pierre had whispered at the last moment, "but I start my rounds in my ward at Saint-Jacques Hospital tomorrow. Next Monday, I'll also resume consultations. Bruno the same. You bring him to us at 9:00 a.m. before the first patients, okay? We must not delay getting X-rays done."

In my car, I found the silence heavy. Claire didn't say much, except to point out monuments to Yiorghos, who was sitting in the back and didn't react.

"That's the Alésia church. Pretty ugly, I agree." We drove a bit further. "And there's the Lion of Denfert. Over there is the entrance to the Catacombs. Or the exit, I'm not sure. We go around, and we arrive at Rue Froideveaux. It runs alongside the Montparnasse Cemetery. That's my street. Lucas is going to drop me off and you will continue towards Pasteur, and Rue de Vaugirard where he lives."

She gave me a peck on the cheek, turned around to kiss Yiorghos, and got out of the car. She disappeared into the lobby of her building without looking back. I felt a twinge in my heart. And I was pleased that Yiorghos changed seats to come sit next to me.

On Rue de Staël, I immediately found parking. Not far from the entrance to 174. I left the camping gear in the car, only took out my bag and the rest of our travel provisions, and signaled to Yiorghos to follow. Past the heavy wooden door, we crossed the lobby and began the climb to my eagle's nest. I could see that Yiorghos was struggling with the stairs.

On the sixth floor there was a row of maid's rooms. The last three doors of the corridor were my haven.

"Here is the shower, which I installed in a former broom closet, no one else uses it. There are the toilets, which we share with three or four others. Right across, that's mine."

I felt as if I was rediscovering the place through his eyes. 172 square feet, with a small kitchen corner on the right. My bed on the left wall, a beanbag chair beside it, a table with two chairs in the middle; at the back to the left, the doors of a large closet, and then, near the window, shelves with books in front of them, a board on trestles: my desk. An old dark oak floor, covered by a high-pile white wool rug—well, not really white anymore—and on the walls, ecru burlap. All the moldings bright orange. A poster of Che Guevara, a Picasso dove. And then, a panoramic view of Delphi, and a clay casting of a Greek tragedy mask.

"A *flokati*, Delphi, tragedy... You already loved Greece before going there, huh?"

"As you can see."

"Excuse me, but...We said that tomorrow, we would try to find the Armenian. But if we sleep here tonight, how do we do it? Mind you, I can sleep on the *flokati*."

He had explained during the journey that Sophia, his old Greek nurse from Constantinople—no question for a Greek to say 'Istanbul'—an Armenian through her mother, had a cousin whom she adored in Paris. Yiorghos remembered the address because he had often copied it when addressing envelopes for the letters she sent him regularly. In terms of letters, postcards that she signed with her name accompanied by a heart. Yiorghos remembered him well. He had come two or three times from Athens to Karpathos to see his cousin when he was still living in Piraeus, before moving to work in France at the end of the fifties. Who knows why.

"No way. Look." I pulled out from under my bed the mattress that served as a spare cot.

"Even better!"

We quickly finished the remaining sandwiches, and we laid down, exhausted from the road. I turned towards the wall and I think I fell asleep immediately.

Monday, September 1ˢᵗ

Rising early, I slipped out of my bed from the end so as not to wake Yiorghos by stepping over him, and went down to buy some croissants. To celebrate our arrival. Then, I prepared two cups of Nescafé. The clinking of the crockery woke him up.

Half an hour later, we set off in search of the Armenian. 88 Avenue de la Porte d'Ivry. Poorly connected from my place but I didn't know how to drive there. Yiorghos discovered the subway, the joy of endless transfers, the smells of underground Paris. He was silent or spoke very little. Except when he read "Do not spit" on a sign, which amused him.

"Would Parisians do it otherwise?" he asked with a laugh, before handing his ticket to the ticket-puncher in his booth.

Mr. Mazanian came to open the door for us in his dressing gown. A small bald man, with surprisingly short arms and chubby hands. He did not immediately recognize Yiorghos, but seemed rather pleased when he understood who he was. All three of us stayed in the entrance for a few minutes, enough for me to catch a glimpse of the outdated decor, with its dark furniture and golden tapestries. The apartment smelled musty and there was an odor of cold tobacco and the after-smell of frying. I thought it best to let them talk.

"I'll be back in a little while, okay?"

I wandered around the neighborhood, which was not interesting at all, except for a few Chinese shops and restaurants that were starting to open there, and on my return, exactly an hour later, I found Yiorghos sitting on the threshold of the building, leaning against the wall. Pale. Jaw clenched.

"What's wrong?" I asked.

"..."

"Come on, answer me."

"I can't stay here."

"Why?"

"..."

"Listen, don't explain anything if you don't want to. Let's go home. You'll settle in at my place, that's all. As you know, it's not very big. Still, bigger than a tent or the trunk of the Ami 6," I joked to lighten the mood. "We'll figure it out."

We took the subway again, and when we arrived home, Yiorghos collapsed onto the beanbag chair. I made some more coffee. Maybe because I wasn't asking him anything, and my back was turned to the hot plate, but he blurted out in a hollow voice,

"Το γουρούνι!"

Guessing he wouldn't be inclined to translate, I looked it up in the dictionary. "A pig. Why do you say that?"

"…"

September 8th

On Monday morning, we were early in the courtyard of Saint-Jacques hospital where Jean-Pierre worked as an intern with his friend Bruno. Resourceful as he was, I was sure he had managed to get us a radiology appointment as promised. After a whole Sunday of hesitating, I had decided in the evening to try to convince Yiorghos to seek consultation. Since our arrival in Paris, he was still limping just as much, and I even had the impression that he was finding it increasingly difficult to climb my six flights of stairs. He had initially responded to my suggestion with closed-off silence, even though I had stressed the importance of getting treatment. But when I told him it was a chance to see Jean-Pierre and Bruno again, whom were eager to see him, he had relented.

"Which one is going to examine me?" he asked.

"I don't know. Probably Jean-Pierre. But Bruno will be there."

And indeed, our two friends were waiting for us in Jean-Pierre's office when the nurse let us in. After the expected big hugs, peppered with a few of Bruno's jokes like, "Well, you haven't got a tan yet, my brother," with an exaggerated pied-noir accent, or, "Your hair is growing back, you look cute with your curls, almost as handsome as a Seph!" Jean-Pierre suddenly became serious.

"The radiologist is a friend," he said. "She won't ask any questions. And with her, we'll manage to make sure there's nothing to pay."

"Let's go," said Bruno. "She won't hurt you, don't be scared. I hope you've bought underwear since the trip, *maskeen,*" he added in the conspiratorial tone of a mischievous schoolboy. "Or that uptight Lucas lent you some, because you'll have to show your legs to the lady. She's as pretty as a picture, you'll see, and you never know…"

Yiorghos didn't laugh. He didn't even smile. He never seemed to understand this kind of med-school humor. I had already noticed that.

Rosine greeted us very kindly. She was pretty, indeed. Armenian too, she looked like a squirrel with her auburn hair and sparkling eyes. She motioned us to disappear before leading Yiorghos to the booth.

"You undress," she said while opening the door. "I'll come to open it from the other side." And Bruno burst out laughing again.

"What did I tell you!"

We waited for about fifteen minutes during which we reminisced about holiday memories. They asked me how Claire was. I remained rather evasive, and I heard from the other four. Everyone was waiting to resume their courses. Then Yiorghos came out. A shade paler. He remained silent for a few minutes. Then he went out to smoke in the courtyard. One cigarette after another. I don't know how long it was before Rosine joined us, and she asked me to go see how Yiorghos was feeling. He had seemed very anxious to her.

"Did it go well?"

"She was nice. Too nice, even. I'm not used to everyone taking care of me. You, of all people…"

After a while, Jean-Pierre came to fetch us, brought us back to his office where Bruno was waiting. He took Yiorghos to an adjoining room to examine him. When they came back, they sat down again and Jean-Pierre began to speak in a suddenly very professional tone.

"Yiorghos, my old friend… No need for further examination, the X-rays speak for themselves, and the palpation confirmed it…"

Completely out of place, I wondered if Jean-Pierre would ever learn to drop the 's' from the nominative masculine when addressing a man. Yiorgho… When I turned my attention back to them, Yiorghos, tensely seated in his chair, was shaking his head vehemently, "no." Jean-Pierre, undeterred, insisted,

"It's an essential surgery. Nothing too serious. We re-break the bone that has healed crookedly, set it right, apply a cast, and three weeks later, you'll be hopping around. The left leg, it's just fractured in the tibia, a plaster boot will suffice. But for the right, you can't avoid surgery if you want to dance again one day."

"*Opa*!" Bruno exclaimed.

"As soon as you're out, you'll need to start rehab with the cast on so the muscles don't atrophy. Claire or Lucas will take care of it. After that, we'll move on to a series of deep massages and gym exercises."

"Claire or Lucas, I know who I would choose!"

"Don't be annoying, Bruno. What do you say, Yiorghos?"

"You're all doing too much for me. I can never repay you."

"Who's talking about money? Not me."

"Me neither," Yiorghos replied, with a sad smile.

"We'll take care of everything here," Bruno explained. "The surgeon is a friend, the anesthetist too. For the accommodation and the room, we'll find a solution. It's a convent hospital, the sisters are always ready to help their neighbor. And then, we are their favored Jews. We did a lot of free shifts for them when they had financial problems last year."

Throughout this conversation, I had remained silent. As if I struggled to drive away the images of Yiorghos lying in a white bed, pallid on a pillow, a tube in his nostrils, and an I.V. in his arm. When the future patient went out through the French door for another smoke, I said to the others,

"All this is well and good. But about the money, I don't believe you for a second."

"In our circle, Lucas, we do a *kupa* for these occasions. We pitch in when one of us needs a hand. And then, it's someone else's turn," said Jean-Pierre. "We have fairly wealthy families that we can tax for good causes."

"And if it's never your turn, you don't care! You get it?" added Bruno, smiling from ear to ear and handing me an envelope. "Besides, you're going to take this. It's from Clothilde, Annie, and Nicole. They broke their piggy banks and said there was no reason for you to pay for all the food and cigarettes for Yiorghos while he's waiting to find a job. Jean-Pierre and I, we'll take care of the medical expenses. Samuel, I don't know, we haven't talked about it yet, but you can count on him."

Tears came to my eyes, as if they were a gift for me. Mostly I was moved by their lie about the nuns so as not to embarrass Yiorghos. They were more than friends. I pulled myself together and asked,

"And the paperwork?"

"That, my brother, you'll have to take care of. It's your area: you work for Amnesty, after all. They do get residence permits for political refugees, right? You tell Yiorghos he has to testify about what happened to him. The torture and everything. With legs in that condition, he should be able to convince them. And I'm not even talking about his feet... Rosine told me everything, and then I looked for myself, discreetly. That will also require weeks of massage with a reconstructive balm. You can start before the surgery, and you'll continue when we've removed the casts. So, I was saying, for now, he makes a statement, you find him a lawyer, he applies for a residence permit, even a temporary one, and as soon as he's legal, we operate."

"Yiorghos will never want to do something for his own benefit."

"It's up to you to convince him, my brother," Bruno replied. "Tell him it's for his buddies who stayed there. Besides, it's true!"

PARIS

September 1969

We entered the offices of Amnesty International. A series of small, dark rooms, sparsely furnished and overflowing with files. Madame Colbert was waiting for us. She shook Yiorghos's hand with a smile, then mine, more coldly, it seemed to me. We took our seats on two chairs facing her. A bit plump, her short, bleached hair didn't quite match her wrinkles. She peered at Yiorghos from behind her loud, green glasses, which I found myself thinking were too frivolous for a woman in her position, responsible for collecting testimonies from exiles.

"Mr. Yiorghos Keravnakis, let's get straight to the point. In order for us to help you secure political refugee status, we need to put together a case file. You were imprisoned in Greece, and the brutality of the Colonels' regime is well-documented. However, you will need to provide us with dates, details, and most importantly, a testimony of what you have seen or suffered, which we will hand over to a lawyer. They will be responsible for obtaining the necessary residence permit for you." Yiorghos was silent.

"You speak French, don't you?"

"Yes, Madame."

"You can call me Colette. But then, Lucas, if Mr. Keravnakis, I mean Yiorghos, speaks French, we may not need you. He will have to give me a complete account of what he went through, and he might be more comfortable if we are alone."

"What do you prefer, Yiorgho?"

"…"

Before leaving the room, I turned back to him, and he smiled at me, like a brave child left alone at the dentist's because he is old enough. Colette Colbert had already started to ask her questions. Through the door, I heard the first answers.

"I was born in Karpathos, in the Dodecanese on August 7th, 1949. I am twenty years old. I started studying history but dropped out very quickly. I joined the KKE, the Greek Communist Party known as 'the exterior' at seventeen…"

"And where did you learn French?"

"My mother had me learn at a young age with a French lady who worked at our home. Since then, I've always read a lot in French. My father did not accept my joining the Party, and he threw me out. I arrived in Athens where I joined an amateur theater group. In the evening, to earn a living, I played the bouzouki in a café-restaurant and danced with tourists in Plaka."

"Why were you arrested?"

"Because I was a communist."

"Any particular actions?"

The rest, I already knew. From bits and pieces, while he was in my car, but I had managed to put together the whole story. A group of seasoned activists, musicians like him, had drawn him into planning an attack on a police station in Nea Ionnia, a suburb of Athens. The newly installed military rulers had begun to keep records by neighborhoods of all the potential enemies of the regime, especially those they suspected of being capable of seditious acts. Yiorghos's comrades wanted to steal the records in question and had well prepared their operation, but on the said evening, as they were climbing the wall, they were caught by a patrol. Three of them managed to escape, but Andreas Botzalis and Yiorghos were arrested, beaten up, and taken straight to Bouboulina Street to the Security offices. Since that day, Yiorghos had no news of Andreas, whom he suspected had been deported to Yaros, the Devil's Island. Of the other three, he knew nothing either.

Yiorghos had never confided the rest to me. One evening, after visiting the hospital, as we lay side by side, I turned towards him in the dark and dared to ask a few questions.

"You were crying out in your sleep again last night. Are there things you'd like to tell me?"

"…"

"Even if it's hard, it could do you good, you know."

"…"

"Just tell me what you dream about?"

"The prison."

During this conversation, if you can call it that, I brought up the idea of him testifying for Amnesty International. I could arrange a meeting with an official at the headquarters on Boulevard de la Villette. I was well aware that he probably did not want to revisit that part of his past, but he needed to do it. To build his file for a political asylum request. Amnesty could find him a lawyer and pay for it…

"No."

His testimony would help attack the junta. Combined with others, it would be added to the already damning body of evidence and could help convince Pompidou's government to impose sanctions on Greece to demand a return to democracy.

"I don't believe it."

If he spoke out, perhaps a similar fate could be avoided for others, for those who were languishing at that very moment in the Colonels' jails.

"..."

I was out of arguments, embarrassed by my own insistence and perhaps by the harm I was going to cause him, and thinking of the commitment I had made to Jean-Pierre and Bruno.

"It is everyone's duty to work towards ending arbitrary imprisonments," I continued, "and to stop the torture in prisons. You can't just think of yourself."

He turned on the bedside lamp positioned between his mattress and my bed and looked at me for a long time with eyes that seemed almost black at that moment. The burnt honey was gone.

"To tell is to relive. But because you ask, because you believe in it, I will do it. Make an appointment."

At first, I felt relieved. I had obtained what I wanted. And I told myself it was for his good and the good of others. A few minutes later, the lamp turned off, I suddenly felt oppressed. As if I was going to subject him to something unacceptable. A bit of the gravity with which he had accepted my proposal had seeped into me, like a black tide, and it took me a while to understand what was happening while I tossed and turned in my bed half the night. In fact, I was not unaware of what he was going to have to report. I had cheated, forced his silence, and I was ashamed of it.

I knew that he too, lying in the darkness, was not sleeping.

PARIS

September 12th

Yiorghos's testimony through Amnesty International, signed by his hand, I read much later. When I was searching everywhere for clues that would allow me to find him again... An exact echo of many others, notably the frightening one from *La Filière*, published in France as early as January, which I had immediately obtained. Arrested on October 8th, 1967, Pericles Korovessis coldly recounts his arbitrary arrest and what he endured in prison: beatings, falanga, clubbings, floggings, hangings, sexual abuse... He speaks in particular of a pervert named Gravaritis who was more interested in his body than his confessions. Released in March 1968, like ten thousand others since the coup, he left Greece clandestinely for France. He testified before the European Court of Human Rights, eager above all to explain that his case was far from unique and that torture is "only an extension of the social oppression that exists," as he explains in *Nausicaa*, Agnès Varda's film about the dictatorship of the Colonels.

I secretly photocopied Yiorghos's file and kept a copy for myself. I still can't bring myself to reread it. But my memory has retained every sentence. In conclusion, Colette had noted:

"Struck by sharp pains in the chest, Mr. Keravnakis stopped speaking and I ended the interview. No one can doubt this testimony, corroborated by physical marks that I convinced him (with great difficulty) to show to my assistant Stéphane Perret, who co-signs." And this normally restrained activist had added, in pencil, in the margin. "Lost gaze, clenched jaws, tremors throughout the body."

Colette called me the next day at the clinic where I was interning. The residence permit was going to take three or four months, but the lawyer could immediately obtain from the Prefecture a provisional permit that would allow Yiorghos to look for a job and most importantly, to register for Social Security.

Leaving work, on my way back, I bought a bottle of ouzo, a carton of tarama and one of tzatziki from a Greek caterer on Montagne Sainte-Geneviève to celebrate.

Yiorghos was lying on the bed. He was smoking, his gaze lost in the void. I sat on the beanbag right in front of him and said that I had good news.

"What?"

"Colette succeeded. You're going to get a provisional residence permit."

"Thank her."

"Aren't you happy?"

"And my testimony?"

"The lawyer will submit it to the European Court of Human Rights." Then, after a long silence:

"I haven't said everything, you know?"

"I know."

"No. You can't know."

"Do you want to tell me something?"

"I want to sing you a song. And drink the ouzo."

"We say 'some ouzo.'"

"Unless you drink it all, right? Listen. It's called Ρωμιοσύνη. It's a poem written by Ritsos. The music is by Theodorakis. Before the dictatorship."

"What does 'Romiossini' mean?"

"It's hard to translate. It's Greece, but it's more than Greece. *Romios* is an old word that meant 'Greek' in the Middle Ages. Like *roumi* in the Turkish empire. Ρωμιοσύνη is Greek identity. It's what makes you feel Greek, proud of it. The song talks about the Greece that you carry inside. I'm not saying it well, that's a pity."

"Not so bad. But sing!"

And he sang, his voice muffled. Hoarse. Chopped phrases. Plaintive at first, with elongated notes, deliberately trembling, then more rhythmic, bounding, almost warlike. That night, I didn't catch everything. Some words are rare and difficult. Later, I found the text in a bookstore. I understood that it was a song of revolt. The poem says that "one should not weep for Greekness. You think Greece is hunched over, the knife to the bone and the yoke on the neck. But look! It rises and strikes the wild beast with the harpoon of the sun!" Yiorghos, he had turned it into a sad melody, as if his only energy was that of despair. I thought he might be singing about what he had just lost. It was the first time I saw him cry.

After two or three ouzos, we went to bed, without touching the mezes. In the dark, from his bed, he murmured, "One day, I will go back home."

Early December 1969

Claire had left, slamming the door behind her.

Two hours earlier, she had arrived for the massage. Yiorghos had undressed by himself, not without difficulty, and Claire had begun, as Jean-Pierre had prescribed, with the soles of his feet.

While he had his casts on, for three weeks, I myself had done some physical therapy exercises with him. Gradually, I had made an effort to see him as a patient, and myself as a sort of nursing aide. We were both becoming less and less embarrassed. He, perhaps because his marks were gradually fading. Me, because one gets used to everything. And then I was tired of everyone making fun of my modesty. I needed to practice to be comfortable with my future patients. I followed Jean-Pierre's instructions: I generously applied Eucerin to each scar and welt. That, for me, was the hardest part, because images flashed through my mind, and also because he sometimes clenched his teeth, and I noticed it. Each of us seemed to read what was going on in the other's head. When he extended his palm, I placed a bead of healing balm on it, and without him asking, I would go look out the window because I knew very well what he was going to do with it. We let the product absorb, and then, I returned to massage his back, shoulders, and chest with lavender oil. There, he relaxed, and so did I, even though I struggled with the effort. I also helped him change—no small feat with the two casts—to wash seated, his back supported by two pillows, on a plastic sheet spread on the bed, with a terry towel between his legs. I still often turned away my gaze, and when he noticed, he would tease me gently. Without carrying it out, to help me take things more lightly, he once made the gesture of lifting his makeshift fig leaf, and his laughter erupted. The only time in all those mornings. He looked like a mad dog, head thrown back, teeth shining; his whole body was shaking, and the terry towel almost slipped. I thought back to my dream the first night in France, and my own laugh rang a bit false.

Another day, his eyes sad this time, he confided in me.

"You know, I have a twin brother. Adonis. When we were little, we bathed together, slept together, we never left each other's side. You remind me of him, even though physically, you look nothing like him. I feel good with you, like with him."

"Where is he now?"

"He stayed to live with our mother in Karpathos. He's sick."

"What does he have? What's wrong with him?"

"..."

"Well, tell me?"

"Maybe later."

Then, I brought him the basin full of hot water and the washcloth, he soaped up, and finally, I changed the water so he could rinse off before handing him a towel. I even accompanied him to the toilet across the hallway. I leaned back against him so he could pee standing up, without losing his balance on his two plastered legs when he released a crutch. To be honest, the sound embarrassed me every time.

Now it was time to move on to proper rehabilitation and restore strength to the calves and quadriceps, which had become emaciated from the forced immobilization. Deep massages, and in a few days, real strength training exercises and then, first steps without crutches. Claire had decided to take charge of it. I tried to think that it was better for him.

"It looks like you've given up on Lucas's awful shapeless briefs. This is much better," Claire teased.

"This one was a gift from Samuel. Among other things," Yiorghos had replied, giving me a look that he intended to be complicit.

Did she really need to talk to him about his underwear…? Or mine, for that matter…

Shapeless…

The day before, Samuel had dropped off a big bag at my place. He had piled in a pair of trousers and three of his shirts, a nice Shetland sweater, a few t-shirts of various colors, several pairs of socks, and some new white underwear. Before leaving, on the doorstep, he had said to me,

"I didn't have time to wash everything. Well, everything except the trousers. Check carefully before taking it to the laundry or putting it in water, I don't know how you do your laundry. I always forget something in my pockets."

And he had turned on his heel.

That same evening, before going down to the Laundromat on Rue Lecourbe, I remembered to search the pockets, and I had found a large roll of bills in each.

Bruno had once explained to me that Samuel was richer than all the others combined, but it was still a lot of money—"He doesn't know what to do with his cash, our friend. His parents are loaded and they give him as much as he wants. Not to mention clothes! Mind you, he never hesitates to share. I always let him pay to make him feel less awkward," he had said with a wink.

During the massage, I busied myself in the kitchen corner to prepare Claire and Yiorghos a Greek coffee in the copper *briki* I had found at the Flea Market. For three people, four measures of coffee, only two spoons of sugar so it would be medium sweet as they both liked it, the equivalent of three cups of water, and I had placed the pot on the electric hotplate, focused so that it would never boil. Every time the mixture simmered, I would stir with the spoon, and I let it rise to the edge before hastily removing the *briki* from the heat. Seven times in a row, in the purest tradition, so that the coffee would be nice and frothy. Then, I poured it gently, shaking the handle in my hand, attentive that the foam did not disappear into the liquid, that it stayed on the surface, to make it pretty.

"It smells so good!" Claire exclaimed.

"I taught him well, you'll see, he makes a real old-fashioned coffee. Besides, did you see how his hand is trembling?"

I bit my lip: Yiorghos was now joking around! With me, he was always almost taciturn.

I turned towards them, she was kneeling between Yiorghos's feet, which, in the meantime, she had finished coating with the healing balm that was supposed to finish rebuilding the deep layers of the dermis. She was now attacking the calves. Yiorghos, lying on his back, knees bent, legs apart, grimaced from time to time, but seemed on the whole to enjoy the treatment. He turned his head towards me, a playful glint in his eyes.

"A real champion, this Claire!" he said, "I don't know if you would have done as well."

Charming.

"Why do you think he wanted me to take care of it?" (Lie.) "We are in the same year of physiotherapy studies, but I have already completed one more internship than him. Plus, he doesn't really like fiddling men."

"Fiddling?" Yiorghos repeated.

I was always surprised when he stumbled on a word. His French was so idiomatic, almost too perfect, that I never thought that a term could elude him. Often, I told him that he spoke like a book. Still with a slight accent. No sound errors. Ts and Ks too stressed. Js and Chs a bit hissing, but barely. Especially the Rs that scraped his throat. Probably to make sure not to roll them. A different music.

"It means to touch, to feel, to manipulate," Claire explained. "We say that little ones fiddle with themselves when they discover their pee-pees. That boys fiddle girls in the subway just for laughs. But worse, also that pedophile priests fiddle their students…You see?"

I blushed stupidly, and I hurried to distribute the coffees to give myself something to do.

When I looked up from my cup, Claire had started to massage his thighs. Pretending to look elsewhere, I saw her skilled hands vigorously knead the quadriceps as she moved up, then stop to pinch the muscle with all her fingers, before going back down towards the knee. Several times like that, one leg after another.

"The muscles haven't wasted away too much, it seems. Or else you must have been a real athlete before. Still, if you had less hair on your legs, it would be easier!"

"Your coffee is going to get cold," I grumbled.

They both acted as if they hadn't heard me. I don't know if it was that, or Yiorghos's blissful smile, or Claire's cheerful humming, but once more, I suddenly felt a void engulf me. I thought of my wonderful, reoccurring nightmare where I see myself falling out of bed. Anyway, I got up and announced, with all the casualness I could muster, "I'm going out for a walk."

I wandered around the block, rue de Vaugirard, rue de Staël, rue Lecourbe, rue Ernest Renan, and again rue de Vaugirard. Three, four times in a row. More and more restless.

Worried about what, for God's sake? The same twinge of jealousy as on the boat. Claire and I weren't really dating anymore, but I couldn't stand the idea of them being on my bed together. As if stung by a wasp, I ran to my building, climbed the stairs of the six floors four at a time; I arrived out of breath, my heart pounding as if it wanted to burst out of my throat, I turned the key in the lock precipitously and flung open the door. What was I expecting to catch? Claire, who had probably been lying on the bed just before, jumped up and nervously straightened her hair. Yiorghos, for his part, had not moved.

"Get out, Claire. Right now."

"What do you mean? We were just taking a break."

"Get out, I'm telling you. It's better…"

After Claire left, we remained silent for at least an hour. Yiorghos was still on the bed, while I was slumped on the beanbag. From time to time, I glanced at him and saw the level in the bottle of ouzo he had opened slowly decreasing. Suddenly, he sat up and stared at me for a long time. A drop of burnt honey in his already somewhat blurry eyes.

"Claire had only lain down to rest after the effort. You don't want to admit that nothing happened between us, so I'm going to tell you how I escaped from prison."

After much brooding, I was almost ready to believe him, but that "us" made me grit my teeth.

"I don't see the connection," I snapped back.

"You're going to see it. In prison, there were two kinds of interrogations, ones with a thick brute, Babalis, I think. I called him 'the Beast,' for whom you were nothing but a sack of meat and an ashtray. He would lash out at you, but you didn't really exist. He wanted you to talk, that's all, but he tired quickly. The others were conducted by a strange guy, I think his name was Lambrou, we nicknamed him 'the Serpent,' but I'm not sure. Among themselves, they always used different names or first names, so we would have trouble testifying one day, no doubt. That one had a distinguished, icy air, much less brawny, but in any case, he didn't use his strength. He never tired. He specialized in electric torture, and other things too. He took a lot of pleasure in his work. The chance for him to... How do you say it again?... To 'fiddle'...Sometimes, I thought that even if he asked me for the names of my comrades occasionally, he didn't really want me to give them to him. To keep me on hand..."

'On hand'... I thought of Korovessis and some disgusting descriptions of the perverse cop that had remained vivid in my memory.

"He was always accompanied by a doctor who monitored your blood pressure. A guy with glasses who didn't miss a bit of the show, and who signaled whether they could continue or had to stop for now. One day, he didn't come, and a young man replaced him. 'The Seagull.' Very aristocratic, blond, with big clear eyes, he turned his head away to take my blood pressure and he blushed incessantly, like a novice nurse. He was probably an intern forced to be there, but I noticed that the guards who came to fetch me and take me back to my cell afterwards treated him with respect, especially two new ones who had arrived almost at the same time as him. One night, a guard entered my cell and put a black hood over my head before tying my wrists to rings fixed to the wall, arms outstretched. He went out and someone else approached. There too, I prefer not to tell you what he did… And especially, what he asked me to do for him."

Another swig of ouzo. The voice almost hoarse, the articulation slurred.

"You should only know that… Since then…I haven't wanted to fuck…You say it like that, right?"

The bottle we were passing back and forth was now almost empty. Sweat was running down our foreheads. Yiorghos continued to talk, a bit like a sleepwalker if sleepwalkers spoke.

"So you see, neither Claire, nor the Armenian, nor anyone. I swear it to you…"

"But a woman, that's not the same…" I muttered, as drunk as he was or nearly so, as if I wanted to push her into his arms. As if, all jealousy gone, I would have wanted them to be happy together. To fall from the bed and feel truly abandoned.

"…"

"Was it the young intern?"

"Yes, the Seagull. His real name was Stélios. He came back several nights in a row, sometimes he stayed a long time. That time, all night… In the morning at dawn, I remember seeing the sun rising behind the bars, and the moon that hadn't yet set.

The light was green…It's strange the things one remembers… He removed the hood and untied my hands. He threw himself into my arms, forced me to close them around him, began to cry, and asked for my forgiveness, like a little girl. I couldn't understand anything. I couldn't hate him anymore. In any case, he no longer disgusted me. I thought he was like a wounded sea bird. We stayed like that for a long time, and then he raised his head, looked me straight in the eyes, and told me he had a plan… Later, when they would ask if the interrogation could be pushed further, he would say yes. And the next time, again yes. And again yes. So, I would have to arch my back shaking my head very hard, pretending to choke and faint. Then, he would play the one who panics, and he would convince his boss to have me transported to a military hospital where they had isolated rooms, reserved for such cases. Under his surveillance. He would choose two soldiers he knew well—children of his parents' servants, in fact, who couldn't refuse him anything—and on the way, there would be an accident. He would say I had taken the opportunity to escape. He would hide me in a safe place for a few days to regain my strength, and after that, it would be up to me to manage to leave the country clandestinely. He knew that a few others had managed it, he was sure it would work.

"Why was he crying?"

"..."

"Had he fallen in love with you?" As often happens, dodging the last question, Yiorghos replied,

"Maybe because he knew we would never see each other again." And after a silence, and the last sip of ouzo, "And do you want me to tell you... One more secret? A real secret...I cried too."

October 15th, 1969

One of the nicest days that fall had been the day of discharge from the hospital. Our six Sephs, as we had taken to calling them, were there. Too bad for Clothilde, I guess. They all crowded into the small room, and I struggled to gather the few belongings of our patient. A week after the surgery, Yiorghos had regained some color. He just looked a little tired. Lying under his sheet, he seemed to be wondering about what was to come. Under the white cotton, his two legs were captive in their casts.

"As you know," Jean-Pierre explained, "on the right side, you have only one cast boot that goes up just below the knee, with a heel you can put weight on. Not too much at first. The other one, from the surgery, doesn't have a heel; you shouldn't put it on the ground. The plaster is thicker, and we've brought it up to mid-thigh to keep the bones immobilized properly. I've brought you two crutches."

"I know all this, I've already gotten up to go to the bathroom. Thanks, but I have crutches."

"They belong to the hospital. The others are mine, from when I had a ski fracture. Now, everyone's going to leave. Bruno and I, we're going to help you dress. We might have to cut your jeans to get them over the casts. We'll see... Can you pass me those, Lucas? He's not going to leave in his hospital nightshirt."

"Wait," Nicole exclaimed. "I brought something." She pulled from her bag what appeared to be a ball of fabric, but when she unfolded it triumphantly it turned out to be a wide canvas pant. "Harem pants! Look! I cut the bottom and undid the seams so the casts can fit through. They belonged to my father. I'm giving them to you, Yiorghos."

"See, my friend," Bruno, as jocular as ever, quipped, "My girlfriend didn't want your junk to catch a cold just at the moment when you're going to be able to start using it again. Ah, Parisian women!" The joke was in poor taste, but it put everyone in a good mood. Even Yiorghos, who repeated "Junk?" looking at me, and I mouthed to him the Greek equivalent, wondering where I had learned it. It was often like that, anyway. I knew expressions without knowing where I had picked them up. Especially the swear words. Yiorghos smiled.

Ten minutes later, supported by his two crutches, he moved down the corridor in harem pants and a t-shirt, flanked by his two beaming interns, as if they were the ones who had just accomplished the feat of standing up. After verifying that the discharge papers were in order, they lifted him off the ground to carry him across the gravel courtyard to my car where they seated him on the back seat, leaning against Jean-Pierre, his feet resting on Bruno's knees. I sat at the wheel, Claire got in next to me, and the other four followed on foot. 174 Rue de Vaugirard is less than five hundred meters on foot from the hospital on Rue des Volontaires. I parked on the sidewalk. From a distance, I saw Samuel, Nicole, Annie, and Clothilde approaching. I waved to them to show them my building, in case they had forgotten which one it was, even though they had all been to my place when Yiorghos was in the hospital, before we went to visit him together.

We all met in the lobby. The six floors awaited us. Yiorghos said he would take his time, but he would make it up. Behind his back, Jean-Pierre signaled to me that Yiorghos was crazy, and he made circles with his finger next to his head to indicate that the convalescent might get dizzy before waving and shaking the same finger in a gesture that clearly meant no. I was wondering how we were going to convince Yiorghos when Bruno, as he so often does, saved the situation with a joke.

"A Turkish sultan in embroidered harem pants cannot bother himself with climbing six flights of stairs on foot. I said 'Turkish,' sorry. I meant a Greek prince. Besides, there are no Greek sultans as far as I know."

"You're talking nonsense," Annie snorted.

"I'll rephrase: would His Highness deign to sit upon the portable throne to be prepared by his two eunuchs, Lucas-Pasha and Ali-Samuel? Gentlemen, please!" And he took each of our arms, crossing them. I gripped my left elbow, Samuel opposite me in a symmetrical inverse position.

"Bend down a bit, *Hmar* (that means 'donkey' in Arabic, I don't know the plural. In the Ottoman Empire, slaves all spoke Arabic, right?) You are a sedan chair, remember. Prince Georges, please be seated. Hey, I never thought Yiorghos meant Georges! Clothildatra and you, Annisis (the maids were often Egyptian), you ensure the balance of His Highness, who does not look very serene, but well..."

The two girls complied, giggling.

"Ivan Petrovitch and I, Bronoï, because we are great Russian doctors, you must have noticed our blue eyes and blond hair, signs of our obvious racial superiority over all of you, we cannot stoop to help you. Finally, Ivan-Petrovitch deigns to carry the two crutches. Clara will show you the way and open the doors, and exceptionally, I agree to take charge of His Highness's luggage, in addition to my gear. A bit out of place in our caravan, this backpack, but you won't regret it."

This time, I couldn't help but laugh. Even Yiorghos seemed cheerier as he took his place on his mobile throne. The sad cloud that always veiled his eyes seemed to have vanished.

Our curious international procession began the ascent. Ten times we nearly capsized under the weight, especially when we had to turn, and ten times the girls stabilized us. On the third floor, we gave up our places, despite the fierce protests of Bruno, which ended up bringing out Madame Malmy on her landing, disturbed by the racket and our bursts of laughter. The old lady stared at the procession with a severe eye.

"What a mess!" she grumbled, "These young people will do everything to get attention! And what are these clothes?" she asked, pointing to the sirwal pants. "It's like we're at the Flea Market." Nicole and Annie, without consulting each other, launched into joyful ululations. I stuttered out explanations, trying not to chuckle, and Clothilde came to my rescue. With the tone of a well-bred young lady, she presented profuse apologies.

"You see, Madame. Our friend has his legs in casts. He's just come out of the hospital. We're helping him because he can't go up alone."

"Ah, I understand. I hadn't seen his legs with his... His pajamas. It's good to help one's neighbor. You're good Christians, my children..." Seeing that the general hilarity, which everyone was struggling to conceal, might blow our cover, Yiorghos intervened.

"And you are a very kind lady. I thank you for your understanding."

Perhaps influenced by the role assigned to him by Bruno, or maybe just wanting to extend the joke, he rolled his Rs and deliberately missed his nasal vowels. Madame Malmy smiled at him, but turning to me and lowering her voice, she commented,

"That one has a bit of an accent. We're not at home anymore. You've been hosting him for a while now, haven't you? Don't keep him too long, you never know..."

We finished the climb, Jean-Pierre and Bruno taking care of the burden. My back was in pieces, and I even struggled to lean over the lock. They laid Yiorghos on my bed, and sat next to him. I pulled the mattress from beneath the bed and set it up at a right angle as an extra seat by pushing away the beanbag, which I collapsed onto. Annie and Nicole brought two chairs closer, Clothilde and Claire chose the mattress.

"All right, hey guys, let's have a drink," Jean-Pierre suggested.

"And who thought of the aniseed drink?" Bruno asked, pulling from his bag a bottle, as well as big bags of peanuts and a whole plate of tuna rolls. "It's our ouzo, Yiorghos, you'll like it. Lucas, do you have enough glasses? Fresh water, ice cubes, let's go!"

After serving everyone, he raised his glass towards Yiorghos: "*Le Chaim!*"

"That means, 'to life!' But in Hebrew, 'life' is plural," Samuel explained.

"Because for us, it's one for all, and all for one!" Nicole added.

"Cheers," said Claire.

"Yes, to ours, Γειά μας, and especially Γειά σου, Γιώργο (Yiorgo)."

"Yiassou, Yiorghos," they all repeated in chorus, looking at him.

And then, softly, Nicole began to sing: "*Hinei ma tov u mah naim shevet achim gam yachad,*" and everyone joined in. As if Yiorghos was the only one who didn't understand, Jean-Pierre paused in his singing for a moment to translate: "It's so good, so pleasant, to be seated with you, my brothers!" Yiorghos was visibly moved, his melancholic air had returned. Bruno noticed this, and in a stentorian voice, feigned drunkenness.

"A drinking song," he explained, "If you will. Kind of like 'Knights of the Round Table' in Hebrew. But that probably doesn't mean much to you, I suppose. Oh, we're not at home anymore!" as he said to Lucas's ear for everyone to hear his excellent neighbor! "*Hinei ma tov u mah naim...*"

Once the bottle was emptied, everyone hugged and I accompanied them to the landing. Passing by, Samuel whispered to me:

"I'll come back really soon, okay? Tomorrow, if you like. I'll bring some clothes for Yiorghos. And something to eat. My mother makes an excellent couscous; he should like that."

Taking advantage of the fact that she was last in line, I discreetly tried to stop Claire.

"It would be good if we could talk, just the two of us, right?"

She looked at me with her large green eyes, feigning innocence.

"You mean to decide how we're going to manage caring for Yiorghos. Go ahead, there isn't much to do for the moment with his casts. I'll come back by then, but I'll really take over when they've taken them off."

"I'm not talking about that."

"You have something else to tell me?"

"I don't." I turned on my heels and closed the bedroom door behind me.

While I was tidying up and washing the glasses, Yiorghos said to me softly,

"They are all really nice, all our friends. Claire might have wanted to stay. I'm afraid of being in the way."

"Claire and I, we hardly talk anymore. It's over, I think."

"Because of the boat?"

"No, since the accident in Yugoslavia. I'll have to tell you about it."

"I'm sad for you."

"Forget it. I'll find another one soon," I muttered to hide my emotion.

"As beautiful? As smart? You should make up with her."

"That's none of your business."

"Forgive me. You're right."

And after five minutes of silence, when I didn't know how to apologize for reacting so sharply, he turned to me.

"Sorry, Lucas. I have something else to ask you."

"Yes," I replied quickly, happy to have a chance to make amends.

"I don't think I can go to the bathroom alone yet. And also, I'm too hot with these harem pants."

"Of course. I'll help you. You're right, it must be eighty-five degrees in this room. We've never experienced that in September! Let's get you out of your costume, and head towards the can!"

"Can I borrow a pair of briefs?" Startled. I was in the hallway when the friends had put the harem pants on him. I couldn't have guessed.

"No problem. I have two or three old ones with the elastic all stretched out that I was going to throw away." Eyes fixed on his feet, I helped him out of the harem pants, then pulled the briefs up over his ankles, stretching the leg openings as wide as possible. I pulled them up until he could reach them by pulling on his arms and stood up, turned my back, and said that I was ready for the task, but inside I couldn't say I was…

Later in the night, lying on the mattress because I had convinced Yiorghos to keep my bed until his casts were removed, I cried thinking about Claire.

Marc Amfreville

February 1970

I had an appointment with Claire in Luxembourg Garden, Yiorghos with the physiotherapist. He was already walking much better and had started to gain some independence. Notably, he had met a group of Greek exiles in Paris, who gathered on Rue de Seine, at Melina Mercouri's place. Melina had also been driven out by the junta and had taken refuge in France. I had enjoyed her performances in *Never on Sunday* and even more so in *Stella*. And then I had gone to listen to her a year and a half earlier at the Salle Pleyel. I had been literally galvanized by her hoarse voice and dazzled by her gestures during the show, and I had then sunk into a profound melancholy. It was probably the first time I had felt the sense of exile firsthand. I thought, with that reflexive romantic emphasis which I hate in myself: *This woman is both embers and ashes.* She gave me the first shock of music, live, that penetrated and moved me so deeply. I was dying to meet her, but I would never have dared to ask Yiorghos. I knew that they all spent nights together singing and dreaming of returning home and that they had quickly become very close friends. Yiorghos spoke of her with admiration for her struggle, and also with gratitude, because she had found and given him a bouzouki. He would return it if she wished, but as long as he would play it sometimes for her, he could keep it. And Yiorghos seemed to have no desire to stop. He had brought the instrument home, where he couldn't play it because of the neighbors, but sometimes I saw him get up at night, and sitting on the floor, he would take it in his arms and caress it with infinite tenderness. In addition, Melina and the others had committed to finding him a job in Paris, at a Greek restaurant they knew well. In a few weeks, he would probably start working there as a waiter, and with a bit of luck, if Costas, the owner, took a liking to him, he might play the bouzouki and sing on Saturday nights. She would talk to him about it. How could he have refused anything asked of him by an internationally known actress who had transformed into an icon of freedom, gave concerts, organized rallies, and besieged institutions to fight against the junta? I was happy for Yiorghos but a bit bitter to feel him so fascinated by his *pasionaria*, and sad to see him sometimes disappear from dawn until the evenings when he returned darker than ever. Sometimes he didn't come back at all. Was he sleeping at her place? Had he told her everything? I noticed that my friends and I were no longer his only resort, that he had a life elsewhere, and I was already afraid that one day he might forget us.

Yet, he always remained considerate and friendly. For example, it was he who had convinced me to make an appointment with Claire that day. To burst the abscess, he had said, proud to use an expression he had just learned in a novel or another. Why was he so keen to see us reconcile? I couldn't understand it, but I knew that every time he talked about it, I felt overwhelmed. Perhaps because, beyond the sincerity of his good intentions, if I were to start up this relationship again, he would feel free to leave me alone more often… In any case, I had phoned Claire.

I saw her approaching from afar among the bare chestnut trees of the park. Our favorite spot, near the pony rides where you can overlook the pond. No children to sail their boats, no screams from the playground. With this cold, it was hardly surprising that there were hardly any walkers. We greeted each other with a kiss on the cheek, then Claire sat down on a bench, and I sat down not too close but not too far away either. There was the space of one person between us. Of course, I thought of Yiorghos. A shadow between us.

Claire turned to me. She seemed unlike herself. So pale, the mischievous glint in her eyes extinguished, her lips tight, slightly bluish from the cold. She began to speak, hesitating, her hands between her knees, looking fragile in her gray wool coat.

"Lucas, I don't know why you wanted to see me, since we finished Yiorghos's in-home rehabilitation, but I need to speak to you about two things. Before that, tell me, how is he doing? Is he still living with you?"

"Not for much longer. He's made friends, exiles like himself. They've almost found him a job as a waiter in a restaurant, a sort of Greek cabaret where he should even be able to play the bouzouki from time to time. He's doing well. As soon as he has the means, I think he will find himself a room or a studio. He says hello."

"Good. First, I want to apologize. Not for what happened, nor for what I did after the accident, but for not explaining myself. I couldn't then. I think I can now. But it's hard for me. I'm doing this because I love you very much. Like a friend, but very much." A long silence. She didn't move. I didn't dare take her hands.

"When we found ourselves on the edge of the precipice, you won't believe it but I didn't think we were going to fall into the void. I wasn't afraid. I felt like I was in a movie that I hadn't been allowed to see until then but that I already had in my head, like in a black box. Do you understand?" I thought I didn't, but I nodded my head and smiled.

"Don't smile, please, it distracts me. When I was twelve, my father and brother had a car accident. They were driving along the Saône on a country road, there was a terrible storm, torrents of rain it seems, the wheels skidded, my father lost control of the car and it fell into the river."

"And they are…"

"No. My brother got out. He's the one who told me everything. He escaped through the window, but my father was too big to get through. He drowned."

"How awful! But wait, sorry, I don't understand. The car falls into the river. It was raining. I imagine the windows were up. So how could he have drowned?"

Claire started to cry. Quiet tears that slowly rolled down her cheeks. This time, I managed to take her hands. They were icy.

"Exactly, there, you've just understood everything. If they had stayed at the bottom waiting to be rescued, my father might have made it out too. But rationally, he calculated that they would run out of oxygen or that the water would have flooded the cabin before they were found in that remote countryside, and he forced my brother to open his window to save him. Frédéric refused, he resisted for a good five minutes, my father didn't even scream even though he had spent his life yelling at us. It's probably that calmness that convinced my brother. He did it, but to this day, he thinks he should have waited…That Dad drowned because of him. He never got over it, he lives in a clinic taking antidepressants, anxiolytics, and others. When I go to see him, he only talks about that, he apologizes. He cries all the time. I never thought he was guilty. And you either, I never thought you were responsible for the accident. It seems completely crazy at the moment of saying it, but it's as if, at the moment of the crash, I allowed myself to hate him, finally—To hate you in his place. I know it's absurd. And then, very quickly, I felt that you had to hate me too, that you must stop looking at me with your sad puppy eyes. I would even say that's why Yiorghos turned my head a bit, that's why I kissed him on the boat, that's why I flirted with him while massaging him. Not on purpose, you see. I didn't think about it like that, nothing premeditated, but when I reflect on it, with hindsight, that's what I understand. At the same time, I was attracted. Despite myself. Something a bit crazy about this guy that provokes weird things in me… And then also, I think I was afraid of being in love."

"Scared of falling in love with him? With me? I'm lost now."

"No, not with you, nor with him. You're such an idiot. That's the second thing I wanted to tell you today. And you could have figured it out by yourself. But since you didn't want to see anything, I'm forced to open your eyes..."

That's when, all of a sudden, the lightning struck. I've never understood that expression. A lightning bolt blinds you. You don't see anything, precisely. But for me, at that moment, I was suddenly enlightened. I interrupted her.

"Clothilde..."

"Yes, Clothilde. From the very first morning. Love at first sight, do you know what it is? I pushed away the idea with all my might but I couldn't pretend nothing was happening for long. As soon as her hands touched my shoulders, I shivered like never before, and I felt that she was trembling too. I tried to tell myself 'calm down, calm down,' but I was thinking, 'She's too beautiful, it feels too good.' We kissed behind the rocks, hidden, afterwards we always hid, not out of shame, but so as not to hurt Samuel and you. We maneuvered to sleep side by side; on the boat, we would sneak away as soon as we got a minute. We had agreed to meet at the top deck, it's by chance that I found Yiorghos, and when from above, I saw you were going to climb the ladder, I panicked and threw myself into his arms so you wouldn't find me with Clothilde. I was sure you had suspicions, I had to save her, and save myself in the process. That too, is absurd. But I was acting crazy. At that moment, I thought it was the only solution."

"'Shivered like never before.'" Those words echoed in my head louder than all the others. I had heard everything she said, but that sentence was magnified. It was pounding in my head. Then, the images of Clothilde and Claire started to run through my mind. So many examples of my blindness.

"Why didn't you tell me anything?"

"Out of cowardice, of course. But also because I told myself that if you hadn't seen, it was because you didn't want to see. That you couldn't see. For one reason or another, you needed to continue the comedy of the loving couple, and I had the impression that you would collapse if someone forced you to understand."

"To understand what?"

"To understand that you too, were already elsewhere."

"And where is that, according to you?"

"That, *you* know... Listen, it's a lot for me today. And surely a lot for you too. And besides, it's freezing. We're going to part ways nicely. In some time, we'll talk about it again, if you want. I can't anymore. And then, since now I tell you everything, it's not to hurt you, but I want you to know. Clothilde is waiting for me at home. We've been living together for a month."

I remained slumped on the bench. The grey shadow of the coat drifted away down the path.

Another shadow came to sit beside me, just as a shadow used to in this same garden a long time ago. Not a hallucination, since I know there's no one there. Not a ghost, because I don't believe in them. A presence. But an absence as well. The shadow is there because I know it is no longer here. Like when I was little, I confided my distress to it. I explained that I felt split in two. Part of me admires Claire for her courage, her frankness, even for the love that she dared to live. She must constantly think back on the accident of her father and brother, yet she is a cheerful, sunny girl, not always easy, but generous. Others might have withdrawn into themselves, sunk into their sorrow. But she moves forward, and her story with Clothilde is proof of that. No compromises. A diamond. The other part of me is in pain. I feel abandoned, like at the worst times of my childhood, and I want you to hold me in your arms, need to touch your skin, to nestle my neck under your chin, like the little boy you often consoled. I smell the lavender of your discreet perfume. I hear that little noise you made with your tongue against your palate, tet tet tet, like a squirrel nibbling a nut, to make me stop crying. I feel like you're mockingly gentle with me for not having guessed. Like the fairy godmother laughs at the naivety of Cinderella. Nanny, could you with a magic wand make my heart feel less heavy? Claire is gone, for good. Yiorghos comes to sleep a bit less often nowadays. Without ever an explanation. Of course, it has nothing to do with it, but now that they're not sure to find him at my place, I notice that friends visit me less often. In Greek, Yiorghos once explained to me that there are two words for solitude: μοναξιά and ερημιά. One of them denotes the solitude that one has not chosen. The other is the solitude that you find in a desert, but I can no longer remember which one is which. Surely not by chance. Monaxia and Erimia. In any case, you, my little nanny, you never leave me.

That same evening, three weeks earlier, Yiorghos had asked me how I had come by this room. Probably because he was thinking of finding one for himself. And I had explained that my nanny, who had taken care of me from six months to five years old, was the janitress of this building, that she was still there when I was looking for a maid's room to rent after my baccalaureate, and that it was thanks to her that I found it.

"Why weren't you with your parents when you were little?"

"My mother was ill. Chronic depression."

"I also have two mothers."

"I didn't say that. My nanny died three years ago. I still think about her every day. Her name was Clémence, but I called her Nana, like the Saint Bernard in *Peter Pan*. It might sound silly to you, but often, I talk to her. This morning again, at the Luxembourg…"

"It's funny because my nanny, I called her Noná, which means "Godmother" in Greek. She's been completely deaf since birth, and therefore she has a lot of difficulty speaking."

"I'm really going to end up believing that we're twins."

"You're forgetting Adonis, my real twin. Shall we say Τρίδυμα?"

"Triplets. Tri-di-ma, I didn't know the word, but it's guessable. You only spoke to me once about him. Does he look like you?"

"Like the two raindrops, you say that in French, right?"

"Yes. Do you miss him?"

"It's him I think about every day. It's to him that I talk," he replied, with a fixed gaze.

PARIS

April 11th, 1970

Saturday was the big night. Yiorghos was going to play bouzouki at the *l'Olympie* where he had been working as a waiter for a few weeks. He didn't want us to come and see him until then, so on Wednesday I hid behind a tree in front of the restaurant and spied him through the window. Inside was a small room with a bar, then a large stone archway that opened up into a much larger room with vaulted ceilings and fishing nets hanging on the whitewashed walls. Ridiculous. On each side was a long blue table and several small tables in the middle. At the back was a low stage where the musicians would perform and, just in front, a space that looked like a dance floor, deserted on weekdays or, at least, that Wednesday night. From afar I saw Yiorghos moving between the tables, a tray balanced on one hand, bending towards the customers and distributing the plates. He looked like a big bird in his white shirt and black pants. His gestures were certain, there was a smile on his lips, but with a *je ne sais quoi* of distance. He slalomed with ease between the tables, obviously without the after-effects of his operation. Curiously, I thought of Syntagma Square in Athens, where I had admired the waiters crossing the congested streets from the cafés lining the square to serve the customers on the central esplanade. The same graceful elegance and the same imperceptible reticence, as if these slaves of tourism were saying, "I serve you because I have to eat, but look, I brave the danger, I dance between the cars, I remain a free man."

That Saturday I arrived first, and while waiting for the others with my back to the wall I was able to sit as close as possible to the musicians, at one of the two long tables that Yiorghos had reserved for us. The owner welcomed me warmly as soon as I said my name.

"We start with a guitar," he said, "The electric piano, a drum set, and a single bouzouki. Yiorghos will soon join them. At least, I hope so, because you know, he is not very reliable, your friend. Sometimes, we wait for him all evening, he doesn't come to work, and the next day, he doesn't explain why. Weird, isn't it? And even weirder, I don't dare ask him his reasons…Well, tonight, he has to play, it's not the same. I'm sure he'll be there."

Samuel arrived, gave me a warm hug, and sat down across from me.

Bruno, Nicole, Jean-Pierre and Annie did not take long, and almost immediately, Claire and Clothilde arrived arm in arm. A small twinge of regret. I looked at Samuel and we exchanged a look of complicit sadness. I got up like the others and we all embraced as the first notes began to play. Before the waiter could take the order, Costas returned.

"Yiorghos's friends are my friends. Tonight, all-you-can-drink ouzo for everyone, it's on the house."

"*L'Chaim*, well *Yia mas*," said Bruno, raising a still empty glass.

The waiter appeared with a tray full of small glasses, we each took one and emptied it in one gulp. As he was already starting to refill them, Yiorghos came up to the podium from the back and approached his chair, in the middle of the others. Costas turned to him, two glasses of ouzo in his hand. He gave him one, raised his towards us, and Yiorghos imitated him.

"To the friends of our *bouzoukzis*," the boss shouted before bursting into laughter.

We stood up as one, and from a distance, we made the gesture of toasting. Yiorghos sat down first. I had the impression that his eyes were glistening, but how could I tell under the light of the projector? Anyway, for the first time, I simply said to myself that with that white shirt, his bright eyes and his hair thrown back, he was beautiful. In Igoumenitsa, I had been mistaken in thinking that it was the glow of the sunset that dyed his hair red. Now that it had grown, one could clearly see the coppery reflections in the brown curls. And then, I who said not so long ago that I did not even see the eyes of boys, I was hypnotized by the black agates circled with honey.

They started with two or three tunes that I recognized without knowing the titles, and at the end of each piece, the room that had gradually filled up applauded warmly. Yiorghos kept his head bent towards his instrument, which he held up slightly obliquely—a mysterious dialogue as his fingers glided over the strings. By turns, the notes cascaded in a frenzied rhythm that carried you away, or slowly gutted you out as if they wanted to grab your heart. It was the guitarist who sang, and sometimes I heard Yiorghos accompanying him, in a second, deeper voice.

I noticed that the other long table remained empty and I was worried about it. Why didn't everyone come to the premiere of "our" musician? The friends were enthusiastic, the ouzo was flowing, and everyone was chanting the rhythm, forgetting to pay attention to their empty plates, while large dishes loaded with salads and hors d'oeuvres had magically appeared on the table, and Costas was coming from time to time to urge us to help ourselves.

Suddenly, I saw the door to the street open, and a sort of commotion occurred in the room. All heads turned toward the entrance. Even before her long blonde mane, flowing freely, blazed under the archway, I had guessed. It was her. Followed by her posse of friends, instead of going to her place, she shook Costas's hand between hers, then in turn, those of all the customers who had stood up to greet her. She even kissed some of them. The music had stopped as soon as she arrived, but soon the orchestra started *The Children of Piraeus* in her honor. Yiorghos stood up while playing and bowed his head. I was overjoyed to finally see her, I had dreamed so much of this moment. It felt like meeting the fight for freedom incarnate. But at the same time, a dull anger was rising in me. Why tonight? Why come and steal the show? Of course, rationally, she had gotten him this job, she had made sure he had his chance to act and sing, and I should have known she might come. I just didn't think about it. And to read Yiorghos's admiration and appreciation in his eyes before that respectful greeting made my blood boil.

In the voice of a child being taken to a puppet show, Nicole shouted,

"Melina! Melina!"

Feeling awfully embarrassed, I saw the woman turn her head towards our table and give Nicole a bright smile before staring at us, one after the other. Then feeling even more embarrassed, I realized with a few seconds' delay that she was walking towards us, and more precisely, towards me. Still standing, she lit a cigarette, stared at me for a long time and, without taking her eyes off me, pulled a chair to my side. She took my hands, with the same gesture that a moment earlier had seemed so theatrical, and that now made me flinch with emotion. She bent down until she almost touched my cheek with her forehead and in a husky voice she whispered,

"I know who you are. I don't say thank you."

She stood up, followed by all the stares from the audience, and walked to the podium. She grabbed the microphone with one hand and with the other hand she put her hair up, fingers spread, in a star-like gesture. I immediately regained all my prejudices. She was going to sing, to draw the spotlight to herself. She addressed the musicians, and I identified the title of a Greek tune that I knew well, which surprised me, precisely because it was a *zeibekiko* without words. The first notes rang out: a virtuoso prologue, to which Yiorghos immediately gave his all.

The fingers of his left hand jumped up and down on the neck, while those of his right hand alternated without apparent break and at a dizzying speed between plucking and strumming. Just as the melody itself was about to begin, the actress held out her palm and signaled to the musicians to wait.

The audience held its breath. In French, she addressed the already captivated spectators:

"We have here tonight a group of young French people who have pulled a Greek boy from the Junta's prisons. They took risks for him. They took care of him, and welcomed him home as a brother. This Greek is Yiorghos, one of our two bouzouki players, and I know that you all already admire his talent. But he asks you to excuse him. For a *zeibekiko*, he will put down his instrument because he wants to dance for those who saved him. I explain to the French: usually, when he dances a *zeibekiko*, a Greek forgets everything. He dances only for himself. He expresses his pain and his revolt with all his soul. It is never for someone else. It is the opposite of a show. But tonight, Yiorghos wants to dance for Lucas and his friends. He wants to give them this gift because in Greece we do not thank those we love."

Yiorghos put down his bouzouki and stood up. I couldn't be sure, but I could have sworn he was the most surprised in the room. He seemed to be thinking, fighting the urge to sit down again, then he looked at Melina, and he looked at us in turn.

"For Lucas, Samuel, Jean-Pierre, Bruno, Nicole, Annie, Claire and Clothilde."

Then he lowered his chin and jumped on the dance floor.

His arms slowly spread and rise, hanging from the sky by invisible chains. His head sinks between his shoulders. The first notes of the melody resound, played by the second bouzouki, soon joined by the guitar, then the piano. His glance becomes fixed. His feverish eyes seem to want to rise behind his thick eyebrows to hide their madness. Suddenly he leaps on the spot. His arms come back down horizontally like a pendulum and, with slow steps, he starts to stagger, like a drunken sailor, like a glider trying to balance itself. And then, whereas the bouzouki repeats more and more quickly the same heavily punctuated phrase, the throbbing tempo seems to impose itself on his whole body, and his feet mark several crossed steps. He hesitates still one moment before taking off, his palms caress his belly, then, pushed by an invisible force of which he becomes intensely conscious, he starts to twirl, carried by the rhythm and raised by the music.

I believe several times that he is really going to fly away, or to collapse. Old images of his injured feet and legs flash before my eyes. I am afraid for him. I tremble as he trembles. Suddenly, I realize that Melina has come down from the stage and has gone to crouch at the edge of the runway. Head down, she beats the rhythm by clapping her hands. I can hear her bracelets clinking. Several of her tablemates join her, sit on their heels, and imitate her. Like a sleepwalker, I leave my chair, approach and kneel down in turn. From the corner of my eye, I see that the "Six Sephs" and Claire have done the same, also driven by an irresistible impulse. My head is spinning.

At the bend of a chord, here is Yiorghos on his knees, arms extended sideways, as he collects himself. Then a second later his elbows wrap around his chest before unfolding abruptly, as if he wants to seize the air for a moment and make a sinuous way between the clouds by following it with a sudden slowed movement. His palms tense up, his hands flutter, then they tighten and he snaps his fingers to accompany a new sudden collapse of his knees, which touch the ground. He lifts himself up while releasing the tension of all his muscles, lands on his feet, and retreats backwards, head hidden, like a bird huddling under its wing.

He approaches me. Instinctively, I lean forward and lower my head. I see his foot lift off the ground and feel his stiffened leg fly over me, brushing my hair as it passes. As I have seen others do many times in Greece to express their admiration, I pound the floor with my open palm. I hold back my tears. And I know I'm not the only one. His shoulders broaden, his back spreads, he catches his breath and lunges again, both index fingers raised before he tucks himself into an imaginary nest. Swan song: his chest erect, he whirls, jumps once again, higher than ever, before falling down, legs stretched in a split, the neck broken, the nape offered.

Nobody has the bad idea to applaud. Everyone returns to their place. Bruno shakes his head, amazed. Jean-Pierre pats his shoulder, Samuel pats mine before sitting down again. Nicole has reddened eyes and Annie hugs her. Clothilde and Claire move away towards the end of the table, taking each other by the hand, and I would swear that they are shivering. The Greeks also go back to their chairs, Melina in the middle of them, visibly overwhelmed. Yiorghos is back on the platform. Our eyes meet. But his image is blurred.

Until late in the evening, the dances follow one after another. Several of the gang try the *hassaposerviko*, a rather simple step with a fast rhythm, with varying degrees of success. Jean-Pierre makes a fuss because he confuses the moves with those of the *hora* that he learned in the kibbutz the summer before our meeting. Bruno, on the other hand, is perfectly at ease during his first attempt, accompanied by two Greeks he seems to have known all his life, before attracting the four girls to the dance floor and improvising as a teacher. Claire is obviously the most gifted of the group, and Clothilde seems quite clumsy beside her. The dancers follow one another. The plates fly throughout each *zeibekiko*, and a waiter rushes in to sweep up. Only Melina at her table, Samuel and I at ours, do not get up once to dance. We are simply too shattered. At Costas's request, supported by encouraging applause, she reluctantly agrees to sing and I sense that her reluctance is genuine. The lyrics of *Kaymos* that she yowls, the infinite sadness of this music that Yiorghos plays with the bouzouki while accompanying her voice with harmony in the chorus, all blend and rise together to form waves that crash against a dike. I translate as I can the words for Samuel without being able to hold back the tidal wave that overwhelms me:

> *Long is the shore,*
> *high the wave,*
> *deep the pain,*
> *harsh the regret.*
> *The river in me is bitter, it is the blood of your wound...*
> *And from this blood, the kiss on the lips is more bitter still.*

"Why are you crying? You're not the only one who loves, you know?" I'm drowning, and the tenderness in Samuel's voice finishes me.

PARIS

April 11th, 1970

Drunk on music, my eyes full of Yiorghos's dance, I returned alone from the Olympie. Never had the six flights of stairs seemed so arduous. I tried to think that I had overindulged in alcohol but couldn't convince myself. My cluttered room felt empty. Mechanically, I pulled the mattress from its hiding place and laid down on it. Why not simply go to bed in my own bed? Hands behind my head, I closed my eyes. Images from the evening passed by. Yiorghos at the microphone. His hands on the bouzouki. His gaze. The leaps and twirls. A whirling dervish. I laughed to myself, thinking that I had just compared him to a Turk; he probably wouldn't have liked that. An anchorite. I was no longer sure what the word meant, but there is solitude in it. Monaxia or Erimia. The one that Yiorghos defended or the one he imposed on me by not being here tonight. At the corner of the mattress, I found a bottle of ouzo, and I thought I might as well finish it. Even when he had addressed us, calling out our names, even when it was above my head that he had flown his leg, there remained in him a part that was inaccessible. "Eagle of the ice, falcon of the desert," sings Phaedra to Hippolytus in Dassin's film. As if the gift of his dance, akin to a thank you, kept me at a distance, but without his wanting to. I was both chosen and rejected. He probably couldn't give more. I felt a violent desire to console him. A wave of tenderness and helplessness. The words of a Greek song that he had translated and taught me during our conversation classes came back to me, oddly, in French: "So that we may share the pain, halves between you and me..."

At the same time, I realized that the pain of exile cannot be shared. Even though I couldn't quite articulate it clearly— probably the ouzo—I sensed that to approach what the loss of a country can represent, one must have been at home there. And in my case, France had never made me throb. I didn't even feel like I belonged here. Because of my father, no doubt, who had emptied it of meaning without filling the void. I curled up in a ball on my bed. I would never be his twin. I came to hate this Adonis whom I didn't know. With Melina too, I had started to feel jealous. And even with Claire. In fact, I had to admit it, I wanted to be unique. When he had confessed to crying when leaving his Seagull, I had felt a great discomfort. Quickly replaced by indignation. How, even if he had saved him, could he regret being separated from someone who had participated in the torture, who had hurt him physically and forced him to unspeakable acts? I had to stop thinking, let these images disappear. Two swigs later, I felt a hand brush my hair, and another unbutton my shirt to gently massage my stomach. I undressed completely and continued to caress my body, forcing myself to imagine that these hands weren't mine, that I wasn't alone. Obstinately, I tried to think of Claire, but pleasure did not come.

PARIS

April 17th, 1970

Yiorghos had come to pick me up after my intern shift at the clinic, right at 5 o'clock as if he was afraid to miss me.

"I've found a maid's room, at 55 rue de Babylone. Not as nice as yours, but I like it. I want to show it to you. Right now, I have to be at Olympie at six o'clock, we're rehearsing new pieces for tonight. If you want, you can come by later, listen to some music, I'll save you a table, and as soon as I'm done, we'll go back together."

"Nice, yeah. But I have to have dinner with Samuel at Saint-Michel. I'll come, but late, just before you get out. Is midnight okay?"

"Okay, see you later."

And before I had time to offer him a coffee, he had disappeared.

A week without news, I hadn't even had the chance to tell him how much we all loved the evening, and there, out of the blue, he appeared on the sidewalk. I was touched that he remembered I worked on Saturdays and that he thought to tell me he was leaving. At the same time, it was the least he could do. What was I going to do until midnight? Why had I made up that story about dining with Samuel? In fact, I could do something else, find a real evening out with friends and forget our appointment. No question of being at his disposal. He just had to snap his fingers, and I obeyed like a circus dog. At least that's what he thought. I wouldn't go. He'd finally realize that I hadn't come and that would teach him a lesson. If he hadn't forgotten that I was supposed to pick him up.

At exactly midnight, I arrived in front of the restaurant. I hadn't tried to contact anyone. I had wandered from my place to the Invalides, then I had crossed the Seine, walked along the docks of the right bank to Châtelet, then Sully-Morland, Pont Sully, around the Île Saint-Louis, the second arm of the Seine, up Boulevard Saint-Germain counting my steps so as not to be early, and finally, Rue Grégoire de Tours… Olympie. No echo of music. The window was dark.

I let myself fall onto the steps, legs heavy from my marathon. Head between my knees to recover a bit. I felt two fingers tap on my skull as if knocking on a door.

"We had practically no one tonight. We finished early."

My heart leapt with joy. Yiorghos was standing in front of me. Just like in Igoumenitsa on the first day. He had waited for me.

"Shall we go? Here, I got you a pita and a bottle of water." How did he know I hadn't eaten? He extended his hand to help me up. I took the pita and water, as if to admit that I had lied, but especially because I was starving and thirsty.

We went up Boulevard Saint-Germain, turned onto Rue de Rennes, then veered towards Sèvres-Babylone. I had cramps in my legs. The six floors were a real ordeal.

"Your legs seem to hurt a lot?"

"I've been walking all evening."

I blushed at my confession in the dim light, but he probably didn't notice. The room was indeed smaller than mine, with a skylight instead of a window, a bed, and a table on which lay remains of a sandwich, an open toiletry bag, sheet music, and a black pencil. Pinned to the wall was a photo of him, younger. A radiant smile. Eyes a little crazier, maybe. An untamed Appaloosa. In the background, a woman in black, probably his mother. I approached, examined her closely before going to sit on the bed.

"You like my room?"

"Yes. We can do something with it. If you want, I'll help you paint it."

"No."

"No, you don't want to paint, or no, you don't want my help?"

"I don't want to settle down."

His jaws were clenched and he was gazing into the void. In his eyes, I saw Greece: the sea, rocks, pines on a cove. To pull him out of his sadness, I asked, a bit mockingly,

"You hang portraits of yourself now? Is that your mother behind you?"

"Yes, but that's not me, that's Adonis."

"The resemblance is incredible. How did you find this photo?"

"Sophia sent it to me. Do you remember when you received a letter addressed to you, with a sealed envelope inside? Because it came from Greece, you understood it was for me."

I remembered that letter very well and how hard it had been for me not to ask him what it was about.

"You never told me how she got my address."

"I had written to my mother. It was Sophia who replied. Well, she put that photo in an envelope."

"It wasn't very prudent of you to give out my address."

His eyes darkened even further. Then he shook his mane as if to dispel his thoughts.

"You saw me dance the other night."

"Yes, it was beautiful. And it was also very moving that you dedicated that *zeibekiko* to us."

"Shh! Say no more. Look. I want to show you something."

He took a few steps back. I thought he was going to start dancing again. I saw in my mind him leap as if jumping onto a stage, then jump into the air and land in a full split. Without taking his eyes off me, he began to unbutton his shirt and take it off. Using one foot and then the other, he took off his shoes, then rid himself of his socks. One by one, all his clothes flew off. I felt uncomfortable, my pulse quickened. Like an antique statue on its pedestal in a museum, he slowly turned around, his arms outstretched. I wouldn't have been surprised to see him holding a lightning bolt or a trident. An incongruous thought crossed my mind. Bruno said, laughing, "Well, the advantage of having spent a few months in the shade is that he doesn't have tan lines on his butt!" And suddenly, I understood. What Yiorghos was showing me was that there was nothing to see. His back was almost smooth.

He turned around and gently ran his hands over his shoulders, his chest, his sides, they went down to his thighs, and ended up flat on his stomach, just below the navel. His eyes shined. In my head, the images blurred. I saw again the stripes, the burn marks. I thought back to the hours when I applied healing balm to them. Where my fingers tried to erase them. It was as if the film was rewinding. Like during the massages, I imagined the moments when those marks had been imprinted, where that mad violence had been inflicted, and again I shivered.

"You see, I'm healed. Today, if you want…"

Dizziness. I must have heard wrong, he might not have even spoken. In a surge of awareness, feeling like I was clinging to branches, I told myself that maybe I had misunderstood, that he had noticed that I was limping and that he was offering me a massage in exchange for the ones I'd given him. My legs are too skinny, though, and my shapeless underwear… I couldn't imagine his hands on me.

A brief pause. But the spiral of thoughts resumed almost immediately. The Beast and the Serpent waited for me at every turn. The Beast was armed with an iron bar and the Serpent had the electrodes. They both grimaced with a perverse pleasure.

My ears began to buzz, "I prefer not to tell you what he did… and especially, what he forced me to do." The clear eyes. The blond hair. The Gull in tears.

"No!" My vehemence surprised me. I didn't know myself whether I had just shouted my refusal or if I had commanded the images to stop scrolling. The floor stopped wavering. I didn't dare open my eyes.

I caught my breath for a moment but a clammy heat rose to my forehead. Shame, suddenly, of pretending not to understand. The baseness of not living up to his gift. The cowardice of letting him believe that I rejected him. I lifted my head.

"Sorry. I can't even think straight anymore. But…What I feel is that…We're not like that." The light in his eyes went out. He suddenly looked profoundly unhappy. Like a child pushed away when he reaches for an embrace. "I mean that what you're offering, you're doing it for me. Because you think I want it. Me, I don't know, I swear to you, but what I do know is that I can't be the one you force yourself for."

I felt like I was pulling out a tooth. The tooth was loose, so it was better to extract it brutally than to prolong this lingering pain.

Come on, go for it, I say to myself. *Tell him.*

I gathered what little strength I had left.

"I love you too much for that."

June 1970

There was a knock. For a moment, I thought it was him because he hadn't come by for several days, but Yiorghos never knocks. He has kept the key and comes from time to time. Without ever a warning. Sometimes, he even stays to sleep, without asking. We had never spoken again about that memorable night when I had run away without a word. Lost in my thoughts, it took me a few minutes to go and open the door. A few more discreet taps on the panel. On the threshold stood a small woman with white hair, dressed in brown. She wore some sort of pea coat, a beige scarf over her shoulders. I especially noticed the incredible thickness of her glasses, and her grey mustache. With difficulty, she articulated:

"Εγώ Σοφία."

I Sophia…

He would usually come after his shift at the restaurant, bringing food and drink, the unsold items of the evening. I always had ouzo in the fridge. I would quickly answer his questions about what had happened during the three or four days we hadn't seen each other, and then I would listen to him. Most often, he talked about his island, which I ended up feeling like I knew. A large, steep island, with the clearest sea in the Mediterranean, he claimed unabashedly, dry landscapes to the east and even more arid to the north, more humid air on the west coast, alternating between scrubland and pine woods…The port of Pigadia, the villages perched in the mountains, the coves and beaches. He described it like a guide to make me discover it, but I also felt that emotion had to be kept at a distance. The Karpathos of his monologues was never the theater of the life he had led there, it remained aloof from those he loved back home. If his stories sometimes briefly became populated, the figures were barely sketched out, the black scarf of an old woman from Pylès, the colorful skirts of a matriarch from Olympos, the boots of a muleteer from Volada, the gray beard of the priest from Kyra Panayia, the cap of a fisherman repairing his nets in Finiki. It was as if, most of the time, he showed me a book of photographs to convince me to come on vacation. At other times, his voice was sad, the emotion more tangible but, vaguely, I sensed that his nostalgia concealed something. It spoke of the land and the sea, the olive trees and the almond trees, the meadows of tall grass in the spring, it expressed the love he had for his island, but it didn't tell everything. It let me hear the music in the cafés, the warmth of the calls in the streets, the tones of Gregorian chant escaping from the churches, but gradually, I was guessing another pain more relentless than the persistent one of exile. A void that, if expressed, might engulf him.

One evening, I had decided to push him to talk. To relieve him. He had just taught me the second verse of *Kaymos*:

You do not know the cold
Those evenings when the moon doesn't shine
You who do not know
When Charon will carry you away

When he explained to me that in some versions, "those evenings when the moon doesn't shine" is replaced by "those evenings when you're not there," I thought of his brother, of his mother, and I seized the moment.

"Absence and death, is that it? Do you miss your family? You told me you had written to your mother and that she hadn't responded."

"My mother never forgave me for my political involvement and my departure from Karpathos. In the dispute with my father, she took his side. When he died, I returned for the funeral, she didn't speak to me. Above all, but she never told me, she thinks my brother fell ill because of me, that even if he's getting better, he will never completely recover. That there are lasting effects."

"What is wrong with him?

" ... "

"You had said that one day you would talk to me about it. He's my triplet after all."

His long silence, his suddenly completely black eyes, the vein throbbing at his temple. I knew, with the force of a revelation, that his twin was the hidden side of his sadness, the most secret and sharpest pain. The only photo on his wall.

"At seventeen, I tried to escape from Karpathos for the first time. I went to take refuge with cousins in Rhodes. I told only Sophia where I was going, making her swear not to repeat it to my parents. Not even to my brother, because I was afraid they would force him to confess everything he knew. I was at war with my father, we had increasingly violent political disputes. He was a moderate right-winger, but I saw him as a fascist, and he must have thought I was a dangerous revolutionary. In addition, I wanted to play music, act in theater, he dreamed of me becoming a judge or lawyer. One day, he went from threats to blows and I decided to leave. I couldn't fight him. You can't hit your father."

"Were you afraid of having become stronger than him?"

"…It was during that escape that Adonis had a psychotic break. He no longer knew who he was. He stopped eating, stopped sleeping, he screamed like a beast. He didn't recognize anyone, he had nightmares day and night, he saw wild animals that wanted to tear him apart."

"So you came back?"

"He tried to commit suicide by throwing himself off a cliff. It's a miracle he survived. Sophia came to fetch me. All alone, this poor old woman who had never left our island, she took the boat, the bus, she walked miles on foot to my cousins' farm."

"What did she say to convince you?"

"Nothing."

"What do you mean nothing? I imagine she told you everything, well… made you understand."

"No. It was later that she made me understand everything, on the ferry back. At that moment, I was in a field, tending goats to help my cousins. I remember, it was terribly hot, I was sitting in the shade of a fig tree to cool off. I saw her approaching with her gray dress and her straw hat. At first, I thought my father had died. She sat down, and she uttered only two words: Πάμε σπίτι

"Just that, 'We're going home,' and you understood?"

"Yes, well, I think so. I didn't understand exactly what she meant. But very quickly, I guessed something serious had happened to my brother, otherwise she wouldn't have made the trip. I had to go back."

"And you stayed two more years at home?"

"Yes. Until he recovered. At first, he only wanted to talk to me. I spent all my time locked in with him. Gradually, he got better. But between my father and me, the situation was getting worse and worse. I explained it to Adonis. He cried a lot but he was the one who told me I could leave."

"And you never returned?"

"Yes, once. I told you. For my father's funeral. I suggested Adonis follow me to Athens. He didn't want to. He said that away from Karpathos, he couldn't live.

That without me, it would be very hard, but if I came back from time to time, at least once a year, he would cope. The doctor said that he just needed to avoid shocks and stress. I promised, and I left for Athens again."

"And so now, it's been a year."

"A little more. I wasn't arrested right away. And then, a month in prison, and I've been in Paris since September."

"Have you had any news?"

"The photo."

It was the moment of truth to try my Greek, but then I remembered that Sophia was completely deaf. The conversation was difficult. No doubt, I wasn't speaking clearly enough for her to read my lips, but above all, she poorly articulated the few words she did speak, and I didn't catch half of what she was saying. She quickly realized this and chose to mime what she desperately wanted me to understand. I started to talk with my hands too, speaking Greek as little as possible. First, I told her he wasn't there. That he didn't come every day. Maybe tonight, but I wasn't sure. On her part, she was very efficent at asking questions without speaking, pointing at my watch, or circling her finger around its face with a questioning look, or indicating the bed and resting her cheek against her joined hands. I mimicked the gesture to ask where she was sleeping, and she articulated "Mazanian," and I remembered that the Armenian was her cousin. When she showed me four fingers, I guessed she had been in Paris for four days. I asked how she had come by miming a plane, and she confirmed by spreading her arms. I wondered how she had found my address, but without me needing to ask, she showed me the envelope from the letter Yiorghos had sent to her mother. I offered her something to drink and eat, and she only accepted a glass of water. Then, she went to sit on a chair, sitting up straight.

How had she managed this long journey alone? The boat to Piraeus, crossing Athens, the plane to Paris, the metro to my place. All without being able to read and barely speaking. I gave up on asking because, in fact, there was only one question that haunted me. I couldn't find the past tense of the verb 'to come' in Greek in my head, although I was sure I knew it. Instead, I pointed at her, then to the ground, and pronounced "yiati?" Why? Then she answered with one word, showing her heart, and I felt the earth collapse, as when one grasps an obvious fact belatedly.

"Αντώνης."

Adonis.

I don't know how long I remained stunned on my bed, the old woman still sitting on her chair. After a while, as if she had told herself she had to break this silence she couldn't understand, I became aware that she was telling me something. I caught a few snippets and understood some gestures, but I struggled to grasp the overall meaning. She indicated my bed sheets and sketched others in the air laid over her extended arms. Movement of a needle between thumb and forefinger, then fingers fluttering upwards toward the ceiling: they were clearly embroidered by her with bird patterns. Hand on the heart and then open palms before directing them towards me, she explained that it was a gift for me, but apparently, they had been stolen, which she expressed with an eloquent movement of the closing hand while the wrist turned on itself. Fingers folded and rubbing the palm of the other hand made me think of laundry being washed, then large windmills of both arms followed by the universal gesture for money, and with great difficulty, I think I understood that the laundry where she had left the sheets to be washed before offering them to me had not returned them. Brows furrowed, hands spread, fingers touching her mouth and crossing it, the index finger drawing a tear: she was furious and regretted not being able to defend herself to get her sheets back. Palms extended, her fingers rubbing against each other, new tears: she could not forgive herself for coming empty-handed.

How could one remain indifferent to such attention? She had wanted to give me a present. Of course, I was outraged by the theft she had been the victim of. An unscrupulous shopkeeper who had taken advantage of the situation and claimed never to have seen the sheets in question when she had shown her ticket. Or perhaps he had never even given her a ticket, and she hadn't known she would need one to reclaim her property. There surely wasn't a laundry in Karpathos. I couldn't help but be touched by her large sad eyes, which her bottle-bottom glasses seemed to make even more perplexed. By the palpable distress of the foreigner, the vulnerability of the humblest. But also by everything that preceded. No doubt Yiorghos's mother had read her son's letter to her, no doubt it spoke of me. So, at the moment of undertaking a journey that could only frighten her, she who had never been farther than Rhodes, she thought to prepare a gift. One had to imagine that upon opening her suitcase at the Armenian's, before even beginning to look for me in Paris, she had thought to have the sheets cleaned and ironed, which she deemed impossible to offer me wrinkled or soiled… Dignity, sense of honor.

I was moved. All while I admired her, a feeling that didn't come without provoking a righteous anger against the plunderers of this world, when suddenly anxiety reappeared forcefully. I had let myself be distracted, perhaps to protect myself, but it came back like a boomerang, like a pot I knew was about to explode if left a second longer on the fire.

She had come to find Yiorghos. I was going to lose him.

When he arrived, a few hours later, she was still motionless in her chair facing the entrance, and I was still sitting on the bed. The door opened slowly. Yiorghos turned terribly pale on the spot. He didn't say a word. He walked towards her and lifted her in his arms, taking her under the armpits like a child. They looked at each other for a long time. From where I sat, I could only see Sophia's face, her lips and her mustache trembling, her bifocals filling with tears. I got up and left as discreetly as I could.

In the middle of the night, lying in the dark curled up, I heard him turn the key in the lock. In the half-light of the bedroom, in front of the window barely lit by the streetlights, I saw him, as every night when he came home. He would undress, approach the mattress that I pulled out from under my bed, like every night when I hoped he would come back, and he would lie down on the white sheet. His profile was outlined against the orange screen of the curtain. I must have been half dreaming, because from my vantage point, looking down, how could I have made out his face?

"Κοιμάσαι?"

"No, I'm not sleeping."

"I walked Sophia to the Armenian's place. We leave tomorrow. You understand, she came to get me. Adonis had another very serious attack. He no longer knows who he is."

"You can't go back to Greece. You'll get arrested."

"Πρέπει." *It has to be.* An absolute imperative. Something in his tone convinced me that nothing could make him change his mind. He had to redeem what he thought was the cowardice of his flight. He had deserted his country, I had understood that for a long time. Even the exiles who were forced to leave feel guilty in some corner of their mind. But above all, he had abandoned his brother for the second time, which I only understood today. I lay on my back. My chest began to rise, and my heart to pound. Hands were squeezing my throat. Tighter and tighter. I knew they were my own, but I still felt suffocated. I began to cry. Not the silent, dignified tears of a man who is sad and chooses to keep quiet. No. The sobs of a child. Hiccups that made me feel, each in its violence, as if it was the last.

"Ελά να σε πάρω αγκαλιά." I repeated to myself: *Ela na se paro angalia*. I recognized that beautiful Greek word. Αγκαλιά: the embrace. Let me take you in that space between the arms, that has no equivalent in French. That flat area where you lodge those you love as near to you as possible, between your neck and your heart. I did what he asked. I rolled over and let myself slide into his bed. I nestled my head in the crook of his shoulder, overcome by a warm, slightly musky scent that I had never smelled so closely. I guessed that he lifted an arm, and then his hand caressed my hair. Skin to skin, legs intertwined. I let myself be flooded with his warmth and I closed my eyes. The pulsing blood. I felt his desire, and I felt mine.

We remained embraced, motionless. Without moving. For a long time.

Even today, I wonder. I can already imagine the psychologists explaining to me what happened, or rather what didn't happen. "Repression..." I hear Claire laughing loudly, "Because you're too uptight, my poor thing!" I also hear my own voice answering, "Because we were afraid of losing each other." But we are all wrong. At such a moment, why not respond to desire? Especially when it is so compelling. I was perhaps a bit narrow-minded, I had never known any boys, the great sexual freedom had never tempted me, but I am sure I would have obeyed the urgency blindly if the pain had been less intense. We would have "made love" in the literal sense. Like "to create it." To answer the call of the other. To tie bonds between the bodies so that they never separate in the dreams to come. To create memories in defiance of prohibitions. Even my own. But the pain was too harsh. Acute? We were both in too much pain.

Still in the dark, I heard Yiorghos's voice echo against my chest. In my chest. As if he was speaking from inside me. I thought: A Greek dybbuk.

"I haven't told you everything... No, don't turn on the light. Tomorrow you will know it all. Sleep now."

As if emerging slowly from a deep sleep, I felt like I had passed through the wave of excitement that we had not negotiated. The sea was calm. A beyond reached without having crossed any boundaries. A union and a resolution at once. Like two naked twins on the first day, huddled against each other to regain their interrupted intimacy. Like a father and son a few moments after an accident that would soon see them part forever. First fear, then the pain disappears. Faced with danger, they cling to each other to already become one. Self-abandonment, with a smile on their lips, so as not to lose the other.

I no longer know when I truly woke up.

In the morning, when I got up, he was gone.

Nothingness.

I fell to my knees, I looked at the imprint of our bodies on the sheet. Hollows and mounds, broad strokes and fine strokes. Already a story. My eyes turned to the table. There was a letter on it.

Λουκά μου,

I told you about the intern's plan for me to escape. Things did not go exactly as he had anticipated. The Serpent seemed particularly determined to tear confessions from me that day. His gaze was even colder than usual when he asked me his nagging question. "Give me the names of your friends, you little bastard!" And he immediately started to affix his electrodes. Not disposed to engage in his usual preliminary games. Anyway, after the night I had just spent, he wouldn't have gotten much out of me. Out of the corner of my eye, I saw him fiddle with his machine, slowly turning the voltage knob to select one. Behind the generator, I caught a glimpse of Stélios, almost as white as his lab coat, tensiometer in hand. The current passed through me, no doubt already stronger than usual… I knew it was better not to hold back one's screams, it helps to resist. But I didn't want to give that pleasure to the other guy. After a quarter of an hour of almost continuous shocks, he turned to the intern who approached to take my blood pressure. I had the impression that Stélios was trembling. He signaled to continue, and the same routine repeated several times, every quarter of an hour; the Serpent turned his knobs or moved his electrodes, the Seagull gave his green light. After I don't know how many times, the Serpent suddenly seemed to lose his mind. He was increasing the intensity like a kid playing with the throttle of his little electric motorcycle. I really thought I was going to die. It's not just a phrase. I thought it was the end. He was screaming: "But speak, speak, for God's sake!" I was literally lifted off the table, or at least that was the impression I had. Like a flying carpet, I thought to myself. Then something happened: Stélios raised his arm. The machine stopped. I fell back onto the table. And then… Then he approached, and he laid his hand on my forehead, as if to wipe away the sweat. And feeling that contact, I don't know how to say…That gentleness, that coolness, it broke me. No more resistance. I started to cry. Impossible to stop. I sobbed like a child. I couldn't catch my breath. And between gasps, I heard my own voice stammering: Andréas Botzalis, Manos Teriazis, Vassilis Petropoulos, Iannis Alexandrianos. After that, I fainted, without having to pretend, and then things happened as I told you. The transport to the military hospital, the fake accident, the accomplice soldiers carrying me to the planned hiding place. For I don't know how long, I stayed in a fog, a woman tried to feed me, and gave me injections. Vitamins, antibiotics, and calcium injections to repair the bones. I couldn't swallow anything. Just water. I was completely dehydrated. For the medicines, she forced me. Orders from Stélios, no doubt. I never saw him again. Maybe because it was too dangerous, they were watching him since my escape. Anyway, after I don't know how many days, the woman gave me the clothes I was wearing when we met in Igoumenitsa, a small backpack with some provisions, and a little money. She hid me in her trunk and drove me six miles past the Athens exit to a gas station. There I hitchhiked, and you know the rest…

You see, it's a bastard you helped, that you all helped. Tell our friends if you want. You had to know. We don't thank friends, as you know. But we can ask their forgiveness. I had started this letter a long time ago, I finished it at my place last night before coming to meet you. I am signing it this morning. I know you understand that I cannot do otherwise. I take you with me.

Δικός σου, δίδυμε,
    Γιώργος

He wrote Λουκά μου. My Lucas. Δικός σου, δίδυμε. Yours, twin.
I am his brother. He is my dybbuk. My shadow. I am Greek.
Bound. Irreparably.

KARPATHOS

End of June 1970

I was in Piraeus. My plane had landed at Hellinikon airport with a two-hour delay. Annoyed by this setback, I had barely enjoyed the descent towards the sea, even though it was magnificent. A mix of royal blue and emerald green, unexpected colors to observe so close to such a large city. It was 6 p.m., and I already sensed that I would never make it to Piraeus in time to catch the ferry that left at 7 p.m. The luggage was slow to appear on the conveyor belt, and I had no other choice but to take a taxi, decidedly out of my budget, even though, once again, the Six Sephs had been very generous to allow me to leave. Samuel, in particular, who didn't need it, had bought my old Ami 6 well above its price, and Bruno and Jean-Pierre had decided to sublet my room to sleep there between shifts, supposedly to avoid going back to Bourg-la-Reine every night. They didn't need it either, and the proposed sum, even once my rent was paid, would add to my savings, the donations from others, and my parents' help to fund my expedition. The friends had come to Orly to wish me a safe journey, and Nicole, on behalf of everyone, had poured a gourd of water under my feet at the time of departure: "So you come back," she had said, and Annie had explained this old Jewish custom to me: "Because water always returns to its source." I found it beautiful, even if I would have been hard-pressed to say where my source was. Bruno remained curiously silent. Claire was there too, and she had been the last to pinch my cheek in a warm gesture that had brought tears to my eyes just before I crossed the customs barrier. They knew exactly why I was leaving. They had supported me throughout the period following the disappearance of Yiorghos, of whom we had no news.

Apart from their visits, I didn't see anyone, except at the clinic where I was finishing my last internship. Once it was validated, since I had passed my exams—not very brilliantly, but still—I would officially graduate in physiotherapy, which gave me no pleasure since I was far from decided to practice. Every massage, every exercise session reminded me of others and filled me with images, even when the patient was old and ugly. Most often, I wandered the streets, and as much as I tried to avoid the memories, I invariably ended up on rue de Babylone, Boulevard Saint-Germain, or on one bridge after another on the Île Saint-Louis. When you cross the Henri IV bridge from the right bank, you have the most beautiful possible view of Notre-Dame. I watched it shine in the night for a few minutes, a necessary passage, but shortly after I crossed the street to reach the square that overlooks the eastern tip of the island. I jumped over the gate taking care not to be seen. I went deep into the little park, and ran down the stone staircase that leads to the Seine. There, at the tip, there is a tree, an oriental plane, I think. I slipped behind it, right at the edge of the river, and, sheltered by the night, I took off my shirt. "I put my bare back against the bark, the tree gave me strength, just like in my childhood," sings Barbara. I wanted to emulate her but, inevitably seized by dizziness, I backed up against the trunk until the rough bark imprinted on my skin. Some evenings, bending then straightening my knees, I rubbed my back until I felt my skin tear and I experienced a strange relief. On Saturdays, on rue de la Huchette or Montagne Sainte-Geneviève, I sat on the steps of a building almost opposite a Greek restaurant or another, at a safe distance from the Olympie, and I listened to snippets of songs and bouzouki chords while smoking cigarette after cigarette. At home, I slept on the mattress that I no longer bothered to store under my bed in the morning since I knew I would pull it out again in the evening, after having lain down in the middle of the night, after several hours of futile struggle where I had not found sleep. With an empty stomach or nearly so, I was constantly hungry but couldn't swallow anything more than a piece of bread and a few olives. On the other hand, the bottles of ouzo were starting to line up dangerously against the wall. I couldn't say which was winning, the sorrow or the anxiety. I was alternately feverish when waiting for the mail, and completely defeated when the concierge announced that no letter had arrived for me. I had bought a small record player and listened to Theodorakis on repeat, crying over the sad melodies and shivering over the songs of struggle. My favorite record, *The Ballad of Mauthausen*, and in particular that tune that mimics the hypnotic rhythm of the train rolling towards the death camp, left me dazed.

It was Samuel who pulled me out of it:

"You can't stay like this. You have to go look for him. Karpathos isn't the end of the world, and on an island, you're bound to eventually find someone who knows someone who knows where the person you're looking for is."

"Maybe he doesn't want to be followed."

"I don't know about him, but you, I'm sure you do. And that's not the point. It's not just about you and Yiorghos. You have to make sure nothing's happened to him. That's the anxiety you need to deal with. You're the best person for the job, and you need to do it for all of us. Sorry to say it bluntly, but we're all terrified for him. Claire, Nicole, Annie, Jean-Pierre… Bruno is having trouble sleeping and he's joking less and less. It seems even Clothilde talks about him non-stop. As for me… You have to go and let us know. I'm the one asking, but we all feel the same."

I let myself be convinced because I was already convinced. I also needed to feel like I had no choice. Chasing after a boy with whom nothing had really happened was ridiculous. Barely a year of shared life— not even that— a few moments of confusion, exceptional, alright, but not enough to be in this state. Samuel was right, it was the uncertainty of his fate that was unbearable. Going to look for everyone's friend who might be in distress, an activist in danger in a fascist country whom we had saved and adopted, was different. Almost like a customer service of humanitarian solidarity. My poor joke didn't comfort me. Samuel had said "terrified," and his words resonated in me like a tuning fork. They set the tone for my days. I remember seeing him in Igoumenitsa the morning he came back pallid after discovering Yiorghos's back in the shower. After Claire, Samuel had been the first to understand. It was he who had convinced us of the urgency to help him flee. He who today had put my worst fears into words: "Make sure nothing's happened to him." And if he had been recaptured, if he was in prison, if… I had to leave.

The bus took more than an hour to get to the docks, I had just found out. I got into a taxi.

"My boat leaves at 7 a.m. from Piraeus, if you get me there on time, I'll pay double."

Actually, I didn't know how to say "double" but I had shown a bill, then two, with a gesture that the driver had perfectly understood. A mad dash followed on the small, poorly maintained roads that lead to Piraeus, bypassing Athens. He weaved between cars, accelerated on the straights, ignored rights-of-way, and slammed the brakes at intersections, honking every ten meters to scatter a dawdler or a cart.

These suburbs reeked of poverty, most of the houses or small buildings were dilapidated or under construction. Everywhere, there were vacant lots and narrow strips of land overgrown with brush. The streets seemed almost deserted, a beggar at every corner, and all over hideous, crooked billboards. Traffic slowed down near what I guessed to be Piraeus. After a few wider, more upscale avenues, we plunged into alleys so narrow I thought we had lost our way in a recently bombed neighborhood. Gutted concrete facades, peeling paint, rickety chairs on sidewalks in front of gloomy, sparsely frequented cafés. Old men watched us speed by, stroking their mustaches with a puzzled look and flicking their *komboloi* between their fingers. On the cracked asphalt, men and women, almost all dressed in gray or black, hurried home. Despite all the good will and skill of my driver, time was running out. It was ten to seven when we emerged at the port in the already fading light. I had never seen so many boats. The white ferries were lined up in tight rows, and when the driver turned to me to ask which one was mine, I realized I had no chance: I couldn't even remember the name of the shipping company. Panicked, I replied: "Kreta, Karpathos..." before remembering that Crete is "Kriti" in Greek. He smiled, half-mockingly, half-compassionately, and hit the gas again to weave toward what seemed like the most remote part of the port. Confident in his business, he brought me in a few minutes in front of an open gate and stopped before a wooden shack on which a sign I painfully deciphered announced "Lane Line: Milos, Santorini, Crete, Kassos, Karpathos, Rhodes," in Greek and English. Facing the hut, the sea was unusually clear and transparent for a harbor basin, but there was no boat. We were too late. I approached the counter and asked the employee engrossed in his newspaper.

"Karpathos?"

"No boat today. Tomorrow, 7 p.m."

I gave up trying to find out whether I was mistaken or if the schedule had been changed at the last minute. I had carefully written down all the information in Paris... I went back to my taxi. He had guessed everything. Comforting, he told me:

"In Greece, boats always late."

I handed him the two one-hundred drachma bills that I had promised to give him. After all, he had done everything to be on time. He smiled, revealing loose teeth, and only took one bill.

"No boat, no extra money."

I almost forgot to regret this false start. Nothing serious after all. One more day wouldn't make much of a difference to my concerns. I just needed to find somewhere to sleep. I spent the night on a wooden bench in a tiny park squeezed between the avenue that runs along the port and two perpendicular alleys. I was a little afraid of the cops, but no one came to drive me away.

The next morning, I spent several hours wandering aimlessly, unsuccessfully searching for the bar where the anonymous narrator meets Zorba in the novel by Kazantzakis. From time to time, I asked a passerby. Everyone wanted to help but nobody seemed to know. Later, after nibbling on a *koulouri* and drinking a sugarless Greek coffee bought from a street vendor, I started to wander again, this time with the idea of finding the café where Dassin had filmed *Never on Sunday*. No more luck. I wasn't sure of the title in Greek, and when I tried to make myself understood by saying the word *kafénio* along with the gesture of cranking an old-fashioned camera, and then "Melina Mercouri," I could tell that the smiles froze. The looks immediately became evasive, almost scared. Except for one sailor who had stared at me for a long time, putting a finger to his lips. Older and definitely more weather-beaten, he reminded me of Yiorghos. Because of his sad and at the same time warm eyes. Because of the silence. Around 3 p.m., I treated myself to a souvlaki and let the whole ferry deck scene to Brindisi play out in my mind. Once again, I wondered where Yiorghos had found the strength to leap like that, and without transition, I pictured him pirouetting in Paris, on the Olympie's dance floor. I forbade myself to remember seeing him in my room, for more than a few seconds, arms outstretched, slowly approaching me. Not out of modesty, but for fear of the emotion that would overwhelm me if I kept thinking about it. Despite my prohibition, the stairs that I had run down after slamming the door, came back to me, unbidden, each step getting closer to my face, as if I were going to fall at any moment and smash my head.

Around 6 p.m., I returned to the spot where my ferry should have been the day before. This time, it was there. As in Igoumenitsa, a line of cars had already formed in front of the open holds. Via a side gangway, travelers were beginning to board. As I walked up it, I closed my eyes and saw my Ami 6, and even Yiorghos hidden under the blankets in the trunk. I climbed all the successive stairs, up to the highest rear deck, and leaning on the railing, I lit a cigarette and surveyed "this port at the end of the world." The sun was setting rapidly, and on the quay, the last cars were embarking. A blast of the horn and two cigarettes later, I saw the Acropolis in the distance and thought of Claire. I had some regrets, but felt no nostalgia. Now I was happy that she and Clothilde had found each other. Jealousy had given way to envy: I would have liked to have had the same sense of my freedom. Perhaps it wasn't too late.

After a few short-lived attempts to shelter myself, I decided to stay out in the open. The non-smoking lounge was full of noisy children, and the other one, towards which I had instinctively headed, was too smoky even for me. I needed silence, and the cold wouldn't kill me. As the hours passed, only an old priest and a group of hippie-looking young Germans remained on deck with me, sitting in a circle, already on their third joint. They started singing American folk tunes, syrupy and slow, which set my teeth on edge. A little further away, I saw a large family consisting of Greeks of all ages, shaking their heads, whose exact familial ties I tried in vain to guess. I had also noticed a French couple and, seeing that the woman had binoculars on her lap, I approached to borrow them.

"Good evening, I see you have binoculars…"

"How do you know?"

They were indeed the parents of twin girls who, as it happened, joined us as we were speaking, and we burst into laughter. Stupidly, I thought that I hadn't laughed like that for over a month and was immediately overwhelmed by melancholy. Without taking the binoculars that the lady was kindly offering me, I returned to my bench, facing the sea, where the wind began to lash my face and prick my eyes again. Night had fallen, the stars were already twinkling while there was still a hint of daylight. The moon seemed not to want to rise even though I had dreamed of following its silver trail on the sea. With my head tilted back, I waited in vain to see a shooting star, to make a wish.

At Milos, it was too dark to distinguish anything other than the lights of a port that seemed lively, and at Santorini, which even the Greeks no longer call Thira, a few hours later, the *caldera* was already plunged into shadow. Scanning the immense rocky wall that loomed before my eyes, even darker than the night, I imagined the volcano and the endless string of white houses clinging to its slope that one sees on all the tourist posters. Like at Milos, a column of travelers left the boat—the French among others, and I didn't even say goodbye to them – and moved away under the white street lamps of the pier. A few others boarded, but no one climbed up to my deck. To try and fall asleep, I searched my memory for mythological recollections, but nothing came to mind except for that terrible story of the reckless Phaeton. The young god was struck down by Zeus to stop the chariot he could no longer control, and I forbade myself to see an ominous omen in the fate of Phaeton, who was too enamored with freedom.

Upon waking, Crete should be in sight, and I walked to the forecastle to see it first. Along the passageway, I caught a glimpse of two dolphins following the boat. They sped just under the surface, and when they seemed about to overtake us, they turned and popped their heads out of the water to greet us without ever straying from their parallel path. Again, I resisted the tempting associations of ideas and the longing that this perfect movement of companionship aroused in me. A true pair.

Heraklion, Sitia…The ferry skirted the straight coastline before leaving it to veer northwest. Kassos appeared to me as a desolate, uninteresting rock, and anyway, I couldn't see anything anymore. The sun was beating down hard, drops of sweat ran from my forehead and stung my eyelids. Another hour, and the coast of Karpathos pulled me out of my stupor. I approached the rail to try and make out the first outlines, the first reliefs. Since I was already won over, I found the sea more beautiful than anywhere else and decided that these light ochre rocks were sublime. We followed the shore until the southern tip of the island, then headed east with now an almost white sun behind us that made the crest of the waves blinding. Just past the cape, the wind had risen, and the ferry rolled and pitched at the same time. A powerful wind, which did not blow in gusts but swept the sea and the deck without ever stopping, as if resolved to tear me away from the bench to which I clung.

Finally, the boat cruised into a large bay between hills, the wind fell, and I understood that the port was not far. Ten minutes more, and I glimpsed, perched on its cliff to my left, the cemetery that overlooks the city and always seems to be on the verge of diving straight into the sea, Yiorghos had told me, or crushing the port beneath it. The usual slow reverse motion of the boat and we were now facing the docks. Rolling of the capstans, creaking of chains, the ramp lowered, and it was necessary to leave the spectacle to reach the hold and the exit.

I find it hard to admit, but before I was plunged into the belly of the ferry, I was disappointed by what I saw: no white facades, not a cypress in sight, houses of bric-à-brac, mostly two stories, all different, housing terraces with colorful awnings. That too, Yiorghos had said: Pigadia lacks grace, only a few of the buildings are old since neither the Turkish occupier nor his Italian successor bothered to build, arrange, or embellish. At the exit from the embarkation area, women in black are waiting for us, squawking: "Room, Zimmer, Camera..." and I have to make an effort to restrain my bad mood to remind myself that they are working, that they probably have no other sources of income. I approach one of them, who smiles when I say: *Nai, ena domatio, parakalo. Posso kanei?* The sum announced is derisory, even for my tight budget, and I follow her along a street that climbs. I have so little sense of direction that I do not realize that this street borders the esplanade that extends the port, and when after having me climb two flights of stairs by a staircase that ends in a series of metal spiral steps, she pushes the door, crosses the room, and flings open the shutters, I discover the sea below as if slapped in the face. A shock of blue that in an instant reconciles me with my dream. His island will be my island, and I will find him.

July 1970

Three weeks already and nothing. No information, no trace. Nobody seems to know Yiorghos Keravnakis. Apart from the police and soldiers, I think I've questioned everyone I met during the first few days. Mersini, my landlady, has never heard of the name, but she promised to help. I've tried the cafés, restaurants, and shops. I guess I've tried everything, even the church of Pigadia where the orthodox priest, a jovial old man, agreed to consult the baptismal records but without success. I also walked through the cemetery clinging to its promontory above the harbor, deciphering the tombstones. On one of the rare gray days I saw a breathtaking view over the open sea and the hills facing it with their villages submerged in clouds. The priest gave me the precious advice to meet Themis, a Karpathian who knows everyone and runs a bar, the Ouranos, at the outskirts of town. The regulars, besides having their morning coffee or end-of-afternoon beer, gather two or three times a week to listen to good music, and drink ouzo while eating mezes prepared by his old mother. Deep inside of me, I was surprised that a clergyman would give such advice, but I thanked him and the affable priest told me with a mischievous wink that he would probably see me there one of these evenings. Themis knew nothing but, seeing me disappointed, after excessively complimenting me on my Greek, offered me a cigarette and a glass of raki. I sat at his table to chat a little, and he gave me an idea. Had I thought of looking elsewhere than in Pigadia? Sure, the capital was probably the most likely place for what he called "a great family" after my description of a maid, a French governess, and the perfect education of the son, but…

"Yet twins, I would have heard of in Pigadia…You should try the other 'big' towns,"—he laughed at the word alone—"Menetes, Arkasa, maybe, and push up to Olympos to the north. The smaller villages in the mountains, probably not worth it, the rich don't live there much."

"Are there buses?"

"Yes, but not often. Except for Olympos, because there's no road at all. You have to go by boat from Diafani. You'd be better off finding a scooter or a moped. The roads aren't all paved, you'll get a sore backside, but you'll see the country. It's beautiful, our island, you know? Don't grumble, I get it, you're not a tourist and you don't care about the landscape, but on the way…"

"Where can I find a scooter?"

"Listen, if you want, I have an idea because I just so happen to have a waiter who broke his leg last week. A nasty affair, we sent him to Rhodes and I don't know how long he'll be out for. You replace him. Friday, Saturday, and Monday, the evenings when I do '*cabaret*,' you say that in French, right? You help me with the tourists because I don't speak foreign languages. I can't offer you much in terms of salary, but I'll lend you my moped, you can eat and drink whatever you want, and with the tips, you'll pay for the gas, and maybe even more if you work well and the customers like you. If that suits you, you start the day after tomorrow."

I accepted without seeing the vehicle. I probably should have looked at it first. The moped was an old, spluttering, rusted thing, a moped that hadn't been seen in a long time in "Europe," as the Greeks say to refer to everything that lies north and west of their country. The orange paint job was peeling, the exhaust pipe held on by a wire, dented rims, and a large round headlight that didn't light up. But when you are given a horse, you don't look at its teeth, Clémence would say.

I got on it and, duly equipped with a basic map, I began a tour that took me close to ten days in concentric circles and various zigzags: Menetes, perched on its crest, wedged between the rock face and a spectacular drop; Arkasa which I found charmless; the pretty little port of Finiki, where I recognized the fishermen mending their nets that Yiorghos had often spoken of; Messohori, frankly sad and terribly steep on the west coast; Aperi, on the verge of being disfigured by investments from rich Americans rehabilitating their families' houses in their original village... I even pushed up all the way up to Olympos—I had to pay for a passage on a *kaïki* from Diafani, because as Themis had announced, there was no road leading there; a little local Montmartre with ochre, yellow, and even pink or blue walls, with a communal bread oven and three or four windmills perched on the side of a mountain, populated almost only by mustachioed old women in traditional costumes who stubbornly refuse electricity and keep their husbands at home. There I talked at length with a cobbler and bootmaker by trade, musician by vocation, Iannis, who had toured Europe with his amateur orchestra. He had never heard of a young bouzouki player who had a twin brother. I also visited Spoa with its dusty alleys, and finally, on the way back coming from Lefkos I stopped in Pyles, endowed with some magnificent old houses, rich orchards, and a breathtaking view for miles of the sea.

Nothing. Nowhere. No one knew that name. No one had heard of twins around twenty years of age. Only twice did I allow myself a night under the stars. Mersini tended to worry about me, and I forced myself to return even on evenings when I was not working. Above all, I feared the memories of Igoumenitsa. Indeed, that first evening, on a lost cove near a nonexistent hamlet indicated by a sign that read "Amoopi," when I lay down on the sand, Yiorghos was there. I could distinctly see his profile outlined against the Milky Way, clearer than I had ever had the chance to admire it, and I sang for him "Στο περιγιάλι το κρυφό," which he had taught me. "On the secret beach, white like a dove, at noon we felt thirsty but the water was brackish..." When I got to "Our life was a mistake, and we changed life," I cried like a child. I had prevented myself from doing so for too long after each failed attempt to find his trail.

Another time, on the day of Olympos, I arrived by chance on a beach far from any habitation after descending a path of disjointed stones down a steep slope, through a pine forest. The sea was turquoise amidst the needles, and although it was only noon, I decided, once I arrived on the white pebbles I saw below, to stay there until the next morning. I had water, bread, feta, and olives in my backpack. Why not offer myself a break and spend the end of the afternoon swimming among the limestone rocks reflecting on the waves? I needed solitude and silence, without knowing exactly why. Even though my quest was painful, I enjoyed all these conversations with those I met. Everywhere, a warm welcome, attentive ears. Speaking Greek, even poorly, was a real open sesame in a country where most foreigners at best toss out a vague *kalimera* with the wrong emphasis, mumble an unrecognizable *efcharisto*, or laugh upon discovering that *nai* means yes. Still, as much as I worked on it, my accent and my laborious understanding of local expressions betrayed me, and "από που είσαι?" came always too quickly for my taste. Each time I had to specify where I was from, I felt a sense of failure.

End of July 1970

I had started my job as a waiter. Despite some initial apprehension, those three evenings were the best of the week and during the rest of the time I found myself looking forward to them. Yet I also liked the long quiet evenings spent in my room where, sitting at my blue table facing the sea, I watched the night and filled pages and pages of my notebook. I had started with our meeting at Igoumenitsa, still vivid in my memory, and I planned to follow the timeline up to today but, eventually, a scene would burst forth out of order and I decided to write it down immediately.

The Ouranos was first and foremost a terrace with four or five tables, which opened into the room where about ten other tables were arranged. At the back, Themis reigned behind his bar, except for when he came to greet his customers, and the times he disappeared into his kitchen to prepare an omelet with ratatouille or cheese. He did not disdain either to join his two musicians on the small stage or to belt out an old song that everyone sang along to. At the foot of the stairs, an empty space was set aside for those who wanted to get up and dance. There was always Manos, the excellent bouzouki player, and Petros, who played the electric piano and considered himself the conductor, but the singers rotated. An "official" paid for the evening, not always the same, often a certain Dimitris whom I found likeable but a bit of a crooner, and otherwise, the customers who stood up as they felt inspired or whom Themis called to the microphone. A few tourists would occasionally enter, attracted by the music, while they strolled on the shore for a nocturnal walk, but the core clientele were Greeks, either locals or those returning to their island for the holidays. Among the occasional singers, my favorite was Vassilis, a tall man in his sixties, who had been captain of the local football team and who now planted, harvested, and sold his potatoes. He had also been a dowser, which I found magical, and a grouper fisherman in the depths. He had a superb voice and sang without pomp and with a lot of heart, equally successful with Oriental melodies in the rebetiko tradition and cheerful tunes composed more recently that got everyone dancing. Of course, the music of Theodorakis was banned by the junta, but I am sure he would have performed it magnificently. He didn't come every evening, but when he was there, he was immediately asked to take the microphone and he complied with a modest and impish expression, confident in his talent and ready to give his all. I said "with equal happiness," but that's not true. At least not for him. He was never better than when he launched into an ancient lament, his eyes lost in the distance. His voice then seemed to rise from the depths of his belly, he remained completely still as if to let the music emerge. When he had to sing a contemporary tune, on the other hand, he snapped his fingers or tapped the rhythm on his thigh, smiled with all his teeth, and this false joy, this enthusiasm wrenched from his modesty to entertain the crowd, caused me immense sadness. Then our gazes would meet, and I would read in his eyes true kindness, a surge of friendship which he immediately hid under a playful grimace of apology for having sold out to an easy audience.

I had quickly learned to watch for the fingers that were raised to call me and, above all, to spot those who with one hand made a twirling gesture and with the other pointed to a table in the room away from their own. I then had to go see what the occupants were drinking and renew their order at the expense of the one who had just done this double gesture. My vocabulary was more than sufficient to fulfill my tasks, and I was increasingly comfortable accepting a drink, sitting for a few minutes and chatting with regulars, or answering questions from those who had never seen me and who invariably wanted to know my name, find out where I came from, when I had arrived, and how long I intended to stay. I also took advantage, during the musicians' breaks, when Themis played some records at a low volume, to ask in turn if they might know a certain Yiorghos Keravnakis, a bouzouki player. It still sometimes took me an effort to remember that a chin lifting imperceptibly or a small tongue click barely audible against the gums meant no.

I found pleasure in zigzagging between the dancers and tables, and despite my legendary clumsiness, I had yet to break a glass or a dish—which wouldn't have been too serious anyway, considering all the pottery that the audience broke to show their enthusiasm for a dancer or another. When the evening grew late, and I had fewer customers to serve, I would sometimes join in a round dance for the simplest steps which I had quickly learned, framed by two impromptu instructors. In turn, I taught the steps of the dance to the few tourists who wanted to try, and with ouzo's help, I ended up not thinking about anything and fully enjoying these evenings that went by too quickly.

Quite late one night, as he often did, Vassilis approached the table where I was enjoying a break. The remaining customers were all regulars and their glasses were full. Vassilis sat down next to me and signaled to the musicians who started a long bouzouki chord sequence in which I eventually recognized the introduction of *Kaymos*.

"Αυτό το τραγούδι το ξέρεις…"

Yes, I knew that song, but how did he find out? I must have murmured the lyrics when I heard him perform it one evening or another, and maybe even several times. As he began to sing, he put an arm over my shoulder, and with the other hand, he slipped the microphone under my chin. A moment of panic, a few seconds of resistance, but I plunged in. Gently, by pressing his fingers on my shoulder blade, Vassilis was signaling the timing of the reprise because, strangely, one does not hear oneself when singing and the music is not always easy to follow, but soon, I felt "inside" it, and I forgot my stage fright. I was able to raise my head towards the other tables where everyone had stopped drinking or talking to listen to us. When some hummed the chorus with us, I knew we had won them over. I looked at Vassilis and he smiled with his eyes.

Suddenly, from a dark corner of the room, I heard a second voice rising, and for several minutes, I felt that Yiorghos was there. At the last note, the applause crackled but I had a lump in my throat and the faces were blurry. I was no longer quite sure who, the customers or I, was in a fishbowl.

Lying in my bed but unable to sleep, I heard him sing all night. Until morning, he alternated between βραδιά χωρίς φεγγάρι and βραδιά χωρίς εσένα, nights without the moon and nights without you.

August 7ᵗʰ, 1970

I was busy selecting tomatoes when suddenly, raising my head from the stall, I heard what sounded like a peal of thunder—a strange voice, barely audible, struggling to articulate: "ένα κιλό" I recognized it instantly. I turned around slowly; it was indeed her. Then, without really knowing why, I hid myself behind the wall that separates the fruit section from the vegetable section of the small shop, waited for her to pay for her kilo of oranges, and followed her. She continued her shopping, including a long stop at the island's only pharmacy. At the village exit, I saw her climb into her cart and take the road away from the sea towards Afiarti, the small military airport. Considering the pace of her donkey, I had plenty of time to catch up, but I rushed home at full speed to get on my old moped.

A few minutes of anxiety when I didn't immediately see her in front of me on the main road as I expected. I was afraid that she might have turned somewhere before I caught up with her.

But no, further than I thought but still within a short distance, I spotted the cart jolting along the asphalt, and I quickly caught up. With the wind blowing the exhaust smoke away, so as not to lose sight of her, I decided to stay just a few meters behind her. At that junction where, after moving away from the sea since leaving Pigadia, one starts to see the sea below on the left again, she veered right towards Menetes. Four or three miles of sharp turns, a grueling ascent that didn't seem to slow the cart while my little engine grew hotter and hotter. The slope was steep, the heat already intense, and unluckily, not a breath of wind at that altitude. Since there was no crossroad in sight, and therefore no risk of losing her, I decided to stop and take a break, letting my engine cool down after the fourth turn. As far as the eye could see, the arid hills sloped down to the still pale sea in the distance. A few cultivated fields wrested from the dryness here and there, but mostly pastures of short grass, yellowed by the summer sun, and everywhere olive trees climbing the terraces without any concern for alignment, shading the dry stone walls here and there.

I restarted, reached the cart, and began to follow it closely again, with little danger that Sophia would spot me since she couldn't hear my increasingly noisy engine under the strain of the steep climb. At the end of a straight stretch, where a few trees began to grow, I saw her stopping, parking her cart in front of a low wall. She was unhitching her donkey, which was obviously accustomed to the routine and complied without protest, before slowly walking away to seek coolness under a huge fig tree. I also stopped at a respectful distance and watched her, armed with two bottles of water, descending an almost vertical staircase I hadn't noticed before. At the bottom of the steps, the old woman was getting ready to water a bush of carnations. A few steps away was the gate of the Menetes cemetery that one cannot see from the road, or at least not from where I had parked. Perhaps thirty graves, carefully aligned and almost all topped with a more or less rudimentary cross. Beyond the enclosing wall, the valley dropped sharply, all the pale ochre and chamois yellows, and in the distance, the sea blended with the sky.

At the other end of the cemetery, between two tall cypress trees, an unusual shape caught my eye. On a white marble tomb that glittered in the sun, a woman in black was lying down, her arms spread in a cross. I stayed there a long time watching her and did not notice that Sophia had joined me. She stood beside me, her eyes fixed on the stele and the dark form. Without turning her head, she reached out towards me and took my hand. I jumped at this rough touch but was filled with a gentle warmth. Together we watched the woman fold her knees and arms and rise before she walked towards us with a proud step: the mother of Yiorghos, whose silhouette I had studied in the photo pinned in her son's room in Paris. An embodiment of mourning and death at once, as if she had just escaped from the tomb of the one she grieved over without a tear. Her face and hands were parched, she wore a long dress cinched at the waist and cut from a stiff fabric that accentuated her thinness, a scarf tied under her chin, and black stockings. As she moved slowly towards us, I observed the tomb and realized that the slab was not sealed. It bore a raised inscription, white as well: ΑΝΤΩΝΗΣ. Adonis. A shiver ran through me despite the heat and a vein in my throat began to throb.

Sophia let go of my hand. The bereaved lady extended her fingers, and I gently squeezed them, bowing my head respectfully, wondering if she expected a kiss on the hand which would hardly have seemed inappropriate given the nobility of her bearing.

"I am the mother of Adonis. Honored to meet you."

Her French, like that of her son and so many elderly ladies from Greek high society, was absolutely perfect, but marked by a very strong accent with rolled Rs.

"Lucas. My condolences, Mrs. Keravnaki. I did not know your son, but I share your sorrow." The lady's eyes widened for a second then settled on me gravely.

"My name is Alexandra Tsamirou. From my husband's name, Stephanos Tsamiros. Keravnaki was my maiden name. How do you know it? You say you did not know my son? I, I know very well who you are, Sir, since my maid has recognized you."

Why had Yiorghos taken his mother's name? To distinguish himself from his father, no doubt. Unless he had chosen it to go underground. Activists do that sometimes, and he had arrived without papers at Igoumenitsa. In any case, I would never have thought to check.

Sophia had of course heard and understood nothing, but the stern gaze of Kyria Tsamirou must have worried her. Making a diversion, she moved towards the tomb and knelt to place a red carnation on the white marble while crossing herself with the other hand. Her back and shoulders were shaking, and seeing her cry, I could not hold back a tear.

"Come with me, young man. I would be happy to offer you a refreshment or a coffee. My house is just a little further up."

We left the cemetery and I followed her on the road. Sophia lagged behind to untie her donkey and after a few hundred meters, near the church, we turned left to take a staircase rising gently to the top of this hump of a village that is shaped like the back of a camel. We stopped in front of a wall of smooth stones whitened with lime, and Kyria Tsamirou opened a narrow panel in a navy-blue gate. Two cypress trees, even taller than those of the cemetery, guarded the entrance. We crossed a courtyard paved with gray and crimson red tiles and passed a second door, blue as well. Having passed the hall, we entered a room surprisingly cool, with high ceilings and furnished with wood as dark as its beams. My hostess pointed to an armchair and seated herself on another chair facing it, her back straight. I hurried to comply with her gesture, more authoritative than courteous, and, blushing, immediately reproached myself for sitting down before she did.

"My son is dead, as you have understood, but you must know that the tomb you saw is still empty." I immediately imagined that because of his suicide, the priest had not accepted Adonis's burial in his cemetery.

"I know he was ill. But may I ask what happened?"

"Why did you tell me that you did not know him?" I noticed that, like Yiorghos, she did not answer questions. I was searching in vain for how to react when Sophia interrupted us a second time, pulling me out of embarrassment, by bringing us on a copper tray with two cups of coffee, two large glasses of water, and a plate of sesame *koulouria*.

"Help yourself, please. Are you the one who housed my son in Paris?"

"Yes, ma'am."

"I want to thank you."

"Don't thank me. I am a friend. But may I ask what happened?" I repeated, not daring to hope for an answer.

"I do not know much. When he got off the plane in Athens, Sophia let me understand that he was immediately arrested. Probably, the customs officer had photos of the wanted people. He had him handcuffed and ordered two soldiers to take him away." The floor seemed to tilt. Yiorghos, captured. Imprisoned. What were they going to do to him? "Two weeks later, I received an official letter informing me that my son, who had been sought for over a year and arrested at the Athens airport, had been immediately taken to the prison of Yaros, but on the way, he managed to escape by deceiving his guard's vigilance and jumped from the boat. His body, unfortunately, could not be retrieved due to a storm and to this date, has not been found. The death was nevertheless certain given the weather conditions…Condolences, etc…etc… I suspect that in reality, they threw him into the water. Many political prisoners have disappeared in this way since the coup."

Yiorghos dead.

I kept mechanically repeating these two words, with a buzzing in my head and a void in my stomach accompanied by violent spasms. In a sort of semi-consciousness, I realized that I must have uttered them out loud because, looking me straight in the eyes as if I were talking nonsense, my hostess continued in an icy tone.

"I had his grave dug, his name carved, and we will bury him if his body is returned to us one day." The dazzling letters forming a first name on the tombstone blinded me.

"But I don't understand! The grave I saw, that's Adonis's. I'm talking to you about your son Yiorghos."

"Sir, I have only one child. Well, I had only one. Adonis." This woman had still not forgiven her son, she only loved the other, while Yiorghos had braved all dangers to return to his brother. He had been arrested, she had just told me. She believed him dead. Why have the first name of his twin on the tomb? Why did she say that Adonis's grave was empty? I was going mad.

"But his brother, my friend in Paris, the twin of Adonis…Yiorghos?"

"I repeat, sir, I had only one son, Adonis. It was he who was arrested and thrown in jail, he who escaped and whom you took to Paris, he who was recaptured on his return, he whose death the police announced to me, he for whom I had the grave dug." Then, in a softened voice and with a warmer look, she continued, "What I am going to tell you will be a shock to you, but you must know the truth. My son was always ill. Ill in his head, but we had not understood. At seventeen, he ran away from home. It was Sophia who went to find him in Rhodes where he had hidden with cousins who had notified us. When he returned, he was haggard and remained silent, overwhelmed for several weeks, he no longer responded to his name. When he found his voice again, he explained that he had come back to save his twin brother, Adonis, because he knew that he had attempted suicide. He had no brother, I told you, but we remembered, my husband and I, that since he was little, he would sometimes talk with an imaginary character he called his twin. The rest of the time, he was perfectly normal and we thought he just wanted to play. When he came back from Rhodes, the psychiatrist we had come from Crete diagnosed a case of paraphrenia. Do you know what it is?"

"No."

"Neither did I. But the doctor explained everything to us and since then I think I have read everything on the subject. It is a mild form of schizophrenia characterized by specific and sporadic delusions, which leaves the patient in an almost normal state most of the time. It is almost impossible to detect the problem except during the episodes. A slight oddity at most, eyes that are too bright, long silences, sometimes a bit disconcerting behavior, and a fierce need for solitude. I imagine you've noticed…Two years later, he decided to leave again and we let him go. He wanted to do theater and music, and also to get politically involved against the Colonels. The arguments with my husband had become incessant and nothing would have made him change his mind. He settled in Athens, we had no news; I think his father died of grief. Adonis did not even come back for the funeral. I never forgave him. One day, I received a letter from Paris where he briefly explained his arrest, his escape, and his flight from the country. I did not respond, but I sent Sophia to find him. He could not stay on his own in France. I thought she alone would succeed in convincing him to return. Indeed, I was right.

I had not foreseen that he would be arrested again and so soon. I wanted to hide him here. One could say that it's my fault… I should have thought of it. I only knew that he had to come back. That only I could take care of him. It was urgent. I was ready to forget everything. After his detention, a certain Andreas, arrested at the same time as him, came to see me in Karpathos. He told me about the prison, the torture, and… even things that Adonis had suffered because he was too handsome… And that I cannot repeat. He told me that he had never denounced his comrades. Then, for the first time, I was proud of my son."

I was stunned. Devastated. Yiorghos, mad. Yiorghos to whom I, myself, had forgiven everything. Even the long-kept secret of his comrades' betrayal. Besides, who can say that they wouldn't have cracked like him? Even his hasty departure that I believed was explained by his brother's crisis. Everything. Everything but this absence that I couldn't get over and that had led me to undertake this journey. I was ready to embrace him, to pick up things where we had left them that last night. And now, I had embraced a shadow. The image, conjured from his brain, of the twin brother he had invented. Why? No matter how hard I hammered it into my head that he was ill, I couldn't stop thinking that he had lied to me several times. About his father's funeral. About his surname too. About his mother whom he said preferred his brother. But how to know if he believed it himself? The existence of his twin, his suicide attempt, I'm sure he believed in them. Outside of the crisis moments, he could have confessed everything to me, but where did his delusions end? I didn't know his first name, but maybe he no longer knew it either. Only the truth of the marks that I had gradually erased remained, the dance he had offered me, the music of his voice, the memory of that body that I had refused once. And then, our last night, and his letter. The confession of his betrayal. Like a final act of grace so that my hero would become an ordinary man, capable of the worst, and that I would forget him. Unless Andreas had lied to his mother out of charity, and Yiorghos had told the truth. Unless it was she who lied, she who was delirious. But to what extent?

Nothing mattered anymore. From the depths of his madness, he had made me his triplet. In his moments of lucidity, if he ever had any, he still called me "his twin."

Dizziness. I was spinning in an endless abyss until I clung to the only remaining branch, like my old car that had crashed into the only tree on the side of the road in Yugoslavia. He couldn't be dead. He had escaped, he had managed to swim to the shore, he had hidden, he was still hiding. Sooner or later, he would return to Karpathos. I would be there.

I don't remember if I said goodbye to Kyria Tsamirou. I rushed to the door and ran down the road to get my moped back. A violent wind had risen, pushing me from behind with incredible force, tearing me off the ground like a zeïbekiko dancer. While suspended in the sky on my two wheels I forced myself, despite my usual fear, to let go of the handlebars several times on the rare straight paths. I thought back to the tomb of Kazantzakis. Unlike the writer, I had hope, but I was still afraid, I wasn't free, but I was alive. And so was Yiorghos.

I rode to Amoopi. Then, on foot, I staggered down the steep path, stumbling over the stones that rolled under my steps. On the cove, I shed all my clothes and swam straight to the large reef shaped like a sperm whale emerging from the waves and circled around it. The coolness of the water did me good. On the other side, facing the open sea, no construction in sight, no sign of life. I pulled myself up to dry land and climbed the rock where a cormorant had perched. The last ray of sunlight on its steel beak blinded me for a moment. Beyond my vision, nothing but the cobalt sea and the bare rocks. A desert of limestone and pumice that Ulysses could have discovered thousands of years ago and made his own if Karpathos was indeed the Island of the Winds spoken of by Homer.

A mineral solitude that made me realize that I would always be a stranger on this land. But because the twin I had invented was born here, I am now at home under this sky, more than anywhere else.

The sun had disappeared. I dove to return to the cove, already overtaken by the shadow of the cliff. From a distance, I spotted a figure on the shore. Swimming as fast as I could, I made it to the edge and pulled myself out of the waves, stumbling over the pebbles.

He reached out his hand to me. Side by side, we watched the sea, then I turned to him. Our voices mingled to hum *Kaymos*, and I held him in my arms. Under the wind, we were no longer two, but one.

Embrace. Αγκαλιά…

Glossary

8—Nephos: smog

11—Pastèli: sesame and honey confection in bar form.

15—Kaymos: pain, sorrow, melancholy

18—Η πέτρα είναι ο θάνατος, η πέτρα είναι η ζωή μου. I pètra ìne o thànatos, i pètra ìne i zoì mou. Stone is death, stone is my life.

21—Εμπρός παιδιά! Embròs paidià. Onward, children!

23—φίλοι. Fìli. Friends

30—Την Παναγία σου. Tin Panayìa sou. Literally "Your Virgin," in the accusative, complement of an elided obscene verb, this is one of the most commonly used Greek swearwords.

39—Flokàti: unbleached high-wool carpet.

41—γουρούνι. Gouroùni. Pig

42—Òpa. Enthusiastic interjection that often salutes the prowess of dancers.

49—Ρωμιοσύνη. Romiossìni. Greekness.

52—Brìki: copper vessel in which coffee is brewed. "Mètrio": not very sweet.

60—Γειά σου, Γιώργο. Yiá sou, Yiorghos. To your health.

66—μοναξιά. Monaxià. Solitude.

66—Ερημιά: Erimià. Desert.

67—Τρίδυμα. Trìdhima. Triplets

69—Yìa mas: to our health

70—Zeïbekiko: Greek dance performed alone, with no set steps, in which the dancer, traditionally a man, expresses his mood, often melancholy.

71—Bouzouksis: bouzouki player. Traditional string instrument.

72—Hassaposerviko: the simplest of Greek dances, performed as a round dance by several dancers holding each other by the shoulders.

80—Εγώ Σοφία. Egò Sophia. I Sophie

Glossary

82—Πάμε σπίτι. Pàme spìti. We're going home.

85—Κοιμάσαι. Kimàssai. Are you asleep?

86—Πρέπει. Prèpi. It is necessary.

86—Έλα να σε πάρω αγκαλιά. Èla na se pàro angalià. Come let me take you in my arms.

87—Λουκά μου. Loukà mou. My Lucas.

88—Δικός σου, δίδυμε. Dikòs sou, dìdime. Yours, twin.

92—komboloï: a kind of rosary that Greeks and other Orientals make jump and turn between their fingers.

93—kouloùri: small crown of sesame bread. Elinikò: Greek coffee (drink)

93—Kafenìo: coffee (bar)

96—Nai, èna domàtio, parakalò. Pòsso kànei? Yes, a room please. How much is it?

98—Στο περιγιάλι το κρυφό. Sto periyiàli to krifò. On the secret beach.

98—kalimèra: good morning.

98—efcharistò: thank you.

101—Αυτό το τραγούδι το ξέρεις... Aftó to tragoùdi to xèris. This song, you know it.

101—βραδιά χωρίς φεγγάρι and βραδιά χωρίς εσένα: vradià horìs fegàri; vradià horìs esèna. Evenings when the moon doesn't shine; evenings when you're not here.

102—ένα κιλό . èna kilò. Un kilo.

108—Αγκαλιά. Angalià. Embrace.

First Readers

Jayne Anne Phillips (1) USA
Armistead Maupin (1) USA
Laird Hunt (1) USA
Indrajit Hazra (1) INDIA
Abubakar Adam Ibrahim (1) NIGERIA
Amir Ahmadi Arian (1) IRAN/USA
Raynor Winn (1) UK
Janet Hubbard (2) USA
Nazanine Hozar (2) IRAN-CANADA
Brian Evenson (1) USA
Stewart O'Nan (1) USA
Jarred McGinnis (1) USA/FRANCE
Geneviève Brisac (1) FRANCE
Cathy Caruth (1) USA
Cynthia Chase (2) USA
Avital Ronell (2) USA
Philip Barnard (1) USA
Joan Saltzman (1) USA
Susan Bernstein (1) USA
Cristanne Miller (1) USA
Dominique Chevallier (2) FRANCE
Liana Roussi Tzani (2) GREECE
Olivier Cohen (1) FRANCE
Mariette Job (1) FRANCE
André Laks (1) MEXICO
Caroline Pathy-Barker (10) UK
Thierry Bokanowski (3) FRANCE
Sophie Sevdali (2) GREECE
Marie Serda (3) USA
Fenia Antimisiaris (2) USA

Rena Emmanouilidou (1) GREECE
Ilios Willemars (2) NETHERLANDS
Robert Blumberg (1) USA
Sophie Aslanides (3) FRANCE
Frank P. Beninato III (1) FRANCE
Claude Msika (3) ISRAEL
Elie Aslanides (2) FRANCE
Jos. van Wollingen (1) FRANCE
Lida Bitrou (3) GREECE
Myrto Petsota (3) GREECE
Nieko Jongerius (1) NETHERLANDS
Mary Panagiotopoulou (1) GREECE
Michael Sakellis (5) GREECE
Marcel M. Serda (1) FRANCE
Thomas Pughe (2) FRANCE
Christina von Salis-Pughe (1) SWITZERLAND
Timothy von Salis (1) AUSTRIA
Ben Winsworth (1) FRANCE
Petra Pansegrau (1) GERMANY
Christina Manasi (1) GREECE
Jean-Philippe Zermati (2) FRANCE
Catherine Zermati (1) ISRAEL
Antoine Cazé (2) FRANCE
Bettina Kanka (4) GERMANY
Hugo Holland (11) FRANCE
Jean-Michel Ganteau (4) FRANCE
Hélène de Chabert (1) FRANCE
Myriam Amfreville (1) FRANCE
Aggeliki Kiofiri (2) GREECE

First Readers

Nawelle Lechevalier-Bekadar (1) FRANCE
Shiri Kohn (1) ISRAEL
Anna Fyta (3) GREECE
Anne-Sophie Dreyfus (1) FRANCE
Anne-Laure Tissut (1) FRANCE
Patrice Louinet (1) FRANCE
Cécile Roudeau (1) FRANCE
Anne Ullmo (1) FRANCE
Fernando Davin Pérez (2) SPAIN
Laurent Quero Mellet (2) FRANCE
Olivier Paccoud (1) FRANCE
Sylvie Bauer (1) FRANCE
Audrey Bardizbanian (1) FRANCE
Susana Onega (1) SPAIN
Ada Savin (1) FRANCE
Paweł Frelik (1) POLAND
Pauline Lescar (1) FRANCE
Virginie Serraï (2) FRANCE
Manuèle Masset (1) FRANCE
Pierre Bigorgne (1) FRANCE
Anne Besnault (1) FRANCE
Boris Vejdovsky (1) SWITZERLAND
Karin Prinz (1) AUSTRIA
Brian Zielenski (1) TAIWAN
Evita Androulaki (2) FRANCE
Myriam Diallo (2) FRANCE
David Chaouat (1) FRANCE
Paule Lévy (1) FRANCE
Madeleine Voga (4) FRANCE
Sophie Simonelli (1) FRANCE
Evangelos Baxevanis (1) NORWAY

Karine Actis-Borgatti (1) FRANCE
Marie-Christine Lemardeley (1) FRANCE
Lelia Rousselet (1) FRANCE
Agnieszka Soltysik Monnet (2) SWITZERLAND
Élise Amfreville (2) FRANCE
Adrien Le Coënt (1) FRANCE
Sabine Baun (1) GERMANY
Mira Rogulski (1) FRANCE
Ingrid Dimitra Ortner (1) AUSTRIA
Caroline Magnin (1) FRANCE
Romain Garnier (1) FRANCE
Olivia Lewi (1) FRANCE
Dimitris Panaretos (2) GREECE
Alessandro Fico (1) ITALY
Heather Colley (3) UK
James Thatcher (1) UK
Niké d'Astorg (1) FRANCE
Elizabeth Angel Perez (2) FRANCE
Jocelyn Dupont (1) FRANCE
Vincent Broqua (1) FRANCE
Giliane Morell (3) FRANCE
Gregory Boutin (1) FRANCE
Nicholas Manning (1) FRANCE
Myriam Ackermann Sommer (2) FRANCE
Michel Houdiard (2) FRANCE
Alex Fang (1) CHINA
Makana Eyre (1) USA
Anna Street (1) USA
Stéphanie Fonvielle (1) FRANCE
Éric Hoppenot (1) FRANCE

First Readers

Laurent Fauré (2) FRANCE
Valerie Andrews (1) USA
Claire Fabre (1) FRANCE
Jane Werley (1) USA
Mary Moffroid (1) USA
Armelle Sabatier (2) FRANCE
Jacqueline Kanter (1) FRANCE
Jill Moriarty (2) USA
Mary Joye (1) USA
Line Cottegnies (1) FRANCE
Michele Irwin (1) USA
Edouard Marsoin (1) FRANCE
Naomi Berhane (1) USA/FRANCE
Henri Kristof (1) FRANCE
Ben Winsworth (1) FRANCE

Manos Gerapitridis (1) GREECE
Aloysia Rousseau (1) FRANCE
Beatrice Catanese (1) FRANCE
Carine Ramella (1) FRANCE
Marc Abensour (1) FRANCE
Paolo Cassella (1) ITALY
Richard Anker (1) FRANCE
Anne Etienne (2) IRELAND
Christophe Serda (1) FRANCE
Nicolas Lakomicki (1) FRANCE
Anna Galanis Alexiades (1) USA/GREECE
Franck Bolly (1) FRANCE
Gwen LeCor (1) FRANCE